OWNING IT
Stories About Teens with Disabilities

D1529166

OWNING IT

Stories About Teens with Disabilities

edited by
DONALD R. GALLO

CANDLEWICK PRESS

Introduction copyright © 2008 by Donald R. Gallo
Compilation copyright © 2008 by Donald R. Gallo
"Here's to Good Friends" copyright © 2008 by David Lubar
"Tic and Shout" copyright © 2008 by Gail Giles
"Triclops" copyright © 2008 by Julie Anne Peters
"Under Control" copyright © 2008 by Chris Crutcher
"Way Too Cool" copyright © 2008 by Brenda Woods
"Good Hands" copyright © 2008 by Ron Koertge
"See You" copyright © 2008 by Kathleen Jeffrie Johnson
"Fatboy and Skinnybones" copyright © 2008 by René Saldaña Jr.
"Brainiac" copyright © 2008 by Alex Flinn
"Let's Hear It for Fire Team Bravo" copyright © 2008 by Robert Lipsyte

First paperback edition 2010

The Library of Congress has cataloged the hardcover edition as follows:

Owning it : stories about teens with disabilities / edited by Donald R. Gallo
 — 1st ed.
    p.   cm.
Summary: Presents ten stories of teenagers facing all of the usual challenges
   of school, parents, boyfriends, and girlfriends, plus the additional
complications that come with having a physical or psychological disability.
    Contents: Here's to good friends / David Lubar — Tic and Shout /
Gail Giles — Triclops / Julie Anne Peters — Under control / Chris Crutcher —
Way too cool / Brenda Woods — Good hands / Ron Koertge — See you /
Kathleen Jeffrie Johnson — Fatboy and Skinnybones / René Saldaña Jr. —
Brainiac / Alex Flinn — Let's Hear It for Fire Team Bravo / Robert Lipsyte.
         ISBN 978-0-7636-3255-7 (hardcover)
1. Children's stories, American. 2. People with disabilities — Juvenile fiction.
              3. People with mental disabilities — Juvenile fiction.
  [1. People with disabilities — Fiction. 2. People with mental disabilities —
   Fiction. 3. Short stories.]   I. Gallo, Donald R. II. Title.
                        PZ5.O955 2008
             [Fic] — dc22   2007024963

             ISBN 978-0-7636-4661-5 (paperback)

       10 11 12 13 14 15 RRC 10 9 8 7 6 5 4 3 2 1

           Printed in Crawfordsville, IN, U.S.A.

          This book was typeset in Garamond.

                   Candlewick Press
                   99 Dover Street
              Somerville, Massachusetts 02144

             visit us at www.candlewick.com

CONTENTS

INTRODUCTION

This book began with a note passed to me by Darla Wagner, then a middle school English teacher and now an assistant principal in Solon, Ohio, during a workshop on adolescent literature. Earlier, she had asked me what my next short story anthology was about, and I told her I had no idea. Her note to me said: "I need a collection of short stories for Jessica, Cassidy, Eddie . . . who deal with serious illnesses/diseases (brain tumors, cancer, diabetes . . .) and for all the teachers and students who are part of their lives." It was the perfect idea.

UNICEF and other international agencies estimate that there are between 120 million and 180 million disabled children and teenagers in the world. Some are disabled by genetic defects or malnutrition, others by diseases, automobile accidents, or armed conflicts. And while increased attention has been paid to disabled children and disabled adults, the group that has received the least attention is disabled adolescents.

While studies show that disabled teens have the same educational and employment aspirations as nondisabled teens, disabled teens are likely to face more obstacles and exclusions by society in general and to be the objects of physical and verbal harassment by their peers. As a result, a majority of disabled teens suffer from isolation, depression, and low self-esteem.

This collection of stories is one small step in an effort to rectify that. So, thank you, Darla Wagner. This collection of stories is for you and for Jessica, Cassidy, Eddie, and all their disabled peers who seek acceptance and independence in this challenging world.

Although the number of disabilities featured in this book is limited, I hope these stories will serve several purposes. One, disabled teens will be able to identify with these uncompromising characters whose disabilities are like theirs or whose determined responses to their disabilities will strike a positive chord with their own lives and feelings. Two, nondisabled readers will better understand the feelings of disabled teens and, in turn, become more sensitive to disabled peers in their classrooms. Most of all, whether you are disabled or not, the writers and I hope you will simply enjoy reading these stories.

Don Gallo

Everything is under control as far as Brad is concerned.
Is he the only one who doesn't see there's a problem?

Here's to Good Friends

DAVID LUBAR

"Spit out that gum!"

I hate it when teachers shout. What's his problem? I looked up at Mr. Forester, who was huffing down the aisle toward my desk. First period on Monday, you'd think he'd have the decency to let us ease back into the grind. School's enough of a drag without having to plunge right into quadratic equations, the Great Depression, or the use and misuse of the gerund.

"Ratner, spit out that gum right now. I asked you three times. Are you deaf?"

"Me?"

Mr. Forester pressed right up against my desk. "Is there another Brad Ratner in the room?"

"If there is, I hope he did my homework."

I heard some choked-back laughs from around the room. I glanced over at Jordie and grinned. Forester bent forward and got right in my face. "Now."

I pushed my chair away from the desk and walked over to the garbage can. *Patoooee. Thunk.* I love the sound gum makes when you spit it into a can. I wonder if there's some kind of career where I could do that. Wouldn't that be awesome? I could see myself like one of those street musician guys with the wild hair and shaggy beard. Playing the gum can. Yeah. I could set up different cans, with different sounds. Pass the hat. Make enough money to buy more gum. Maybe get famous and be in *Rolling Stone.* Brad Ratner, world's best rhythm spitter. Of course, a beard might be a bad idea, with all that gum.

Crap. Forester was shouting again. I headed back to my seat. Almost tripped, but I caught myself. Maybe I should tie my laces. Not cool, but definitely less trippy.

Forester glared at me and shook his head. "Every day, Ratner. It's getting old."

Yeah, so are you.

At least he left me alone for the rest of the period.

I met up with Jordie in the hall when the bell rang. "You better watch it," he said. "Forester is going to give you detention."

"Nah. He can't. I've got detention deficit disorder."
Damn. That was pretty funny. I let out a laugh as I realized what I'd said. "Yeah, that's it. I've got DDD. Got a
note from my doctor. I even have a prescription for attituderol. They gotta treat me special. It's the law."

"Dickhead." Jordie gave me a push. And then he
forgot all about everything in the world except his
glands because his main squeeze, Carla, was coming down
the hall.

Carla. Yum. She was fine. Hot. Smart. Fun. She had
this body that, if she was made out of cake, you'd eat the
whole thing because it would be impossible to stop after
a couple bites. She reached us and gave Jordie the sort of
hug that's illegal in seventeen states. Lucky man. I think
they're going to be together for life. That's cool. I was
happy for them. After they untangled, she looked over at
me and said, "Oh. Hi, Brad."

No smile. That's the thing. She was hot. But sometimes, for no reason at all, she was cold. Maybe I should
call her Faucet. Wasn't there a Sarah Faucet or something
like that? I could call her Shallow Faucet. But that would
piss Jordie off. And I wouldn't do that to my best pal. I
mean, even though we've been hanging since tenth grade,
he could have dumped me when they started going out.
But we still did lots of stuff together.

"Brad."

"Huh?"

"Did you hear what Carla said?"

"No. Sorry. I was thinking about something."

"She said they added seats for the sold-out show. The extra tickets go on sale tomorrow night."

"For Razor Heart Nine?" That was awesome. They'd just released a new CD. I could play the first part of a couple of their songs on my guitar.

Jordie frowned. "What are you talking about? We saw them last month. Are you spacing out on me?"

"Just kidding." I turned to Carla. "Sounds great."

"We gotta go," she said. She grabbed Jordie's hand and dragged him down the hall toward their second-period class.

"DeepAndDark!" I shouted after them as I remembered which band was coming to the arena.

I headed off to English class. Tripped again. Gave up and tied my laces.

Must have lost my homework when I dropped my notebook. Ms. Tilden wasn't happy about that. I could see a lecture bubbling away in her chest and rising up toward her mouth. But I gave her my charming smile and she gave me some slack. People like you if you smile.

I survived English and headed for algebra II. It would be easier if I could get to my locker after third period. That would be perfect. But my third- and fourth-period classes are in the north wing on the third floor, and my locker is way across the building on the first floor. By the end of fourth period, each minute seems to take an hour to tick off. I can taste the bell.

Ring. Sprung. I pushed through the crowd, surviving the steps because the mob is so packed there's no place to fall. If they played music, it would be a mosh pit.

Thirty-six, eighteen, four. The lock didn't open. Damn. I needed to get in there. I yanked harder and hurt my hand. Damn lock's broke or something. No. Wait. Thirty-six . . . ? That was my middle school number. Four years ago. Why would I even remember it? Stupid mistake. I've had the same lock since way back in freshman year. Twelve, twenty-one, fourteen.

Victory. I got the locker open, grabbed the half-empty Coke bottle from behind my stack of books, checked to make sure nobody was watching, and chugged most of it down. Jesus, that's better.

Back in balance. Life was good. As I put the bottle away and shut my locker, I thought about another swig, but that wouldn't leave enough for later. I'm nothing if not disciplined. I popped a stick of gum in my mouth and cruised down the hall.

There were posters up for class president. It would be cool to be president. I read them as I walked down the hall. Some of them were pretty good. I wondered what mine would say. The election's a month away, in November.

I got to class late. But that's OK. Mr. Breznik is retiring at the end of the year, and he probably wouldn't care if I didn't show up at all.

He barely glanced at me as I walked to my desk. The sound of his voice floated around my head, like background music. It was kind of soothing. I settled into my seat, content. It's amazing how well everything worked out. Except that last bit of fourth period. It's all part of my system. I kept my mind perfectly tuned, like a Lamborghini. Perfectly lubricated, everything in balance, with the formula I perfected last year.

One beer before I leave the house, because breakfast is the most important meal of the morning. But just one, because drunk driving is a bad idea. And one beer doesn't make me drunk. But it doesn't make me flow in perfect harmony with the universe, either.

So I grab the Coke bottle from the trunk—it's a bad idea to have anything up front where it can get you busted—and adjust my blood chemistry before first period. Which makes Forester's droning lectures a lot easier to take. I get my booster shot after fourth period. Another swig or two after eighth kills the bottle and keeps me balanced enough to make it home.

As I strolled out of the building and notched off another day, I was perfectly able to drive. Detention deficit disorder. That really was funny.

* * *

Jordie and Carla were in the parking lot, waiting by my trusty, slightly rusty Civic. He lives way out in the boonies, next to a stunning couple acres of crumpled steel. I'd been giving him and Carla a ride ever since he got a speeding ticket two weeks ago. Before that, Jordie drove most of the time. He was kind of obsessive about that. I guess it's some kind of control thing. I didn't care. I'm just as happy riding in the passenger seat. He's not driving now. He didn't lose his license, but he got his wheels clipped for two months. And he was only going like ten above. His dad, Mr. Talmadge, is real super crazy about safety. He owns a collision and salvage shop. I guess seeing all those wrecks makes him overprotective. Mr. Talmadge doesn't have to worry about Jordie when I'm driving. I never speed. Speed kills.

I hopped behind the wheel, waited for my passengers to board, and took off. It would be fun to drive a cab, I bet. We don't have taxis in Brockford. Too small. But in a city, that would be fun. Zooming around New York or Chicago. Meeting people. Maybe get a rock star in the cab. Get to know him. Hang out with the band at clubs and stuff.

"Brad! Look out!"

I jerked the wheel hard to the right, saving us, then swung left to avoid running off the road. "Did you see that bastard?" I said as the truck vanished in my rearview mirror. "He was way over the line."

I glanced at Jordie, then behind me at Carla, to make

David Lubar

sure they were OK. But just a glance. It's dangerous to take your eyes off the road.

We got to Jordie's house without any more trouble. "How about I drive you home," Jordie said as I rolled to a stop in his driveway.

"What are you talking about?"

"I haven't driven in a while," he said. "Come on. It would be fun."

"Not if your dad found out. And how would you get home?" I asked.

"I could get Todd to pick me up," he said.

I didn't mind letting Jordie drive my car. Anything for a pal. Even if it did seem like kind of a weird request. But before I could say yes, Jordie's older brother, Todd, stepped out on the porch and said, "Dad needs a hand shelving the parts that just came in."

Jordie looked at me, then over at Todd, then back at me. He sighed and said, "Be careful driving home."

"Always." I watched Carla get out of the backseat. Damn. I really wish she liked me. Not like a boyfriend, but like her boyfriend's friend. She and Jordie went inside with Todd. He's a cool guy. He went to Hollywood two or three years ago, and actually worked for a while as a stuntman. For real. He'd still be doing it, but he blew his knee out in a fight scene. So he's helping out with the family business while he works on this screenplay he's writing.

I backed out of the driveway and headed home. Slow and careful. There are a lot of idiots on the road. That truck wasn't unusual. At least once or twice every trip, some jerk swerves too close to me. But I guess I'm just lucky. As always, I made it to my driveway in one piece.

My folks were at work. Dad's an accountant. He twists numbers. Mom's a physical therapist. She twists joints. They both work real hard so that someday they won't have to work real hard. Maybe you have to be an adult to make sense out of that strategy.

I went up to my room and did my chores. Which means I refilled my Coke bottle for the next day. Petrogov vodka is a real bargain. I can get a four-liter bottle for less than my allowance, and that's plenty of cruise-juice to sail me through the week, and have some left over if I want to get a bit of a buzz on the weekend. There are a couple of homeless guys in town who'll buy you booze for a buck or two. I've only been ripped off twice. That's because I'm a good judge of character. The ones who walk the highway, picking up cans and bottles for money—you can trust them. They're hard workers. The ones you have to watch out for are the guys who are so wasted they can't think about anything except their next drink.

I went to the kitchen and topped the vodka off with enough Coke to make it all chuggable. Then I stashed the bottle in my backpack. I was going to do my schoolwork, but I forgot my math book in my locker. So I played Nintendo for a while, practiced my guitar, then took a nap until my folks came home.

It was Monday, which meant Mom picked up lasagna

from the catering place in town. Dad lets me have half a glass of wine with dinner. The first time he did that, Mom gave him a look, but he said, "If he has a little now, it won't be a big deal when he's exposed to it at a party. Face it—kids are going to drink."

"I guess a bit of wine is all right," Mom had said. She gave me the wise Mom look. "But this doesn't mean it's OK for you to drink when we're not around."

I nodded but didn't tell her she was about five years too late with that request. Back in seventh grade, I had this friend, Rob. His dad was always passed out drunk in the living room. Which meant Rob could help himself to whatever was around. Rob was a pal, so he shared. The first time I drank whiskey, I puked in his kitchen sink. But even as I was spitting the sour taste out of my mouth, I wanted more.

Once or twice a week, after school, we'd go to his house and get buzzed, then look through his dad's magazines. I think that's when my grades started to slip. It didn't last long. Rob had to move away after his dad got shot holding up a gas station. So the supply dried up for a while. But by the time I got to high school, booze was everywhere. I got drunk a bunch at first. But then I learned to control it.

"Your father asked you a question."

"What?" I looked up from my lasagna. "School's fine. I had a good day."

Dad nodded. I'd guessed right. Not hard. That's pretty much his one and only dinner question. I like wine. It doesn't have a whole lot of alcohol, so you don't get a fast buzz unless you chug it, which wouldn't be good table manners, but it tastes pretty good.

"You didn't eat much," Mom said when we were cleaning up.

"I had a big lunch." I thought back and couldn't actually remember whether I'd eaten anything at school. Lots of times, I'm not all that hungry. Which is good. Tons of kids are worried about their weight. I guess I'm lucky that way.

Dad stuck his head in the kitchen. "Want to watch a movie?"

"Can't," I said. "Got homework." I grabbed a glass of orange juice from the fridge and took it upstairs. Vitamin C is important. Especially when you mix it with vitamin V.

Tuesday went pretty much like Monday until after school, when I headed for the parking lot. Jordie was staring at my car. I noticed my front bumper was dented on the passenger side. "Damn. Someone hit me in the lot."

"That happened yesterday," Jordie said.

"No way."

He nodded. "When you swerved. You clipped a tree. Don't you remember?"

"Sure. Can't you tell when I'm joking?" I checked out

the fender. It was no big deal. Just a crumple. Even if it had been worse, it wasn't a problem. I could get Todd to swap it for a better one. They've got a dozen cars like mine in the yard, except those cars are wrecked and mine's perfect. Not counting the bumper. And maybe a couple other dings. People were so freaking careless with other people's property. I got in the car, but Jordie and Carla stayed outside.

"We're thinking of walking," Jordie said.

"You kidding? It's, like, three or four miles."

"Nah. It's a nice day," he said. "Besides, it's not that long if we cut through the woods." He gave me a look.

OK. I got it. I figured he and Carla were planning to enjoy nature. "Have fun. Don't fall into the gorge." I laughed. But it's not all that funny. Once or twice a year, someone goes off the road on Springbrook curve, just a quarter mile from Jordie's place, and ends up in the gorge. Or in the pond at the bottom of the gorge. I think the tow truck drivers know the way down there in the dark.

As they started to walk away, I leaned out the window and called after them, "Want me to get tickets for the concert?"

They stopped and looked at each other. "They're expensive," Jordie said.

"Hey, anything for friends. I'll order them tonight. My treat."

They spoke at the same time. "It's not necessary," Carla said. "That would be great," Jordie said.

I stared at Carla. Finally, she said, "That's very thoughtful."

"Awesome." I headed home.

After dinner, I was feeling kind of tired, so I went up to my room and took a nap. When I woke up, I looked at blogs for a while. One of them was all about how great the DeepAndDark concert in Seattle was last week.

Crap. The concert. I checked the clock. It was nine thirty. I already knew what I'd find when I went to the ticket site. Sold out. Damn. Maybe I could score some from a scalper or something. I hated to let Jordie down.

But I couldn't lie to him. "No luck, dude," I told him the next morning. "The tickets sold out in a flash. I guess you have to be connected to get them."

"Hey, no big deal," Jordie said. "Listen, Carla's got to go somewhere with her mom this afternoon. Why don't you come over after school?"

"Sure." I realized we hadn't hung out — just the two of us — for a while. I even let Jordie drive. But we switched right before we got to his place, so his dad wouldn't see. That was kind of sneaky of him, but I understood.

When we got up to his room, he said, "I'm sort of worried about you."

"What?"

"You seem kind of out of it lately."

"I just got stuff on my mind," I said. I walked over to his PlayStation and grabbed a joystick. "Bet I can still kick your butt at Tekken."

"Brad, I'm serious."

"So am I. I can seriously kick your butt." I stared at him and waited.

"Brad . . ."

"Let's play."

"Yeah. Whatever." He grabbed the other joystick. We played for a while, but then I sort of wanted to get home. I'd tried to get Jordie to sneak a drink from his dad's supply once or twice, but he wouldn't do it. He's not real strong in the bravery department.

I wasn't sure why, but I had a feeling he was pissed with me about something. But he'd get over it.

Friday morning, I discovered he was over it big time.

"Guess what I scored?" he asked.

"Not a clue."

"Three tickets to DeepAndDark."

"For real?"

"Yup. Todd got them for me from a friend."

"So we're going?"

"Yeah. The show's at eight. Come over tonight around seven."

"For sure. Want a ride home?"

"Nah. I have a ton of stuff to do. But I'll see you tonight."

This was awesome. The rest of the day passed in a blur.

I got to Jordie's about a half hour early. Carla was already there. I joined them up in his room.

Carla gave me another of her funny looks. I didn't care. I was pumped for the show.

"I got something special for the concert," Jordie said. He held up a bottle.

"Brandy. That's pretty classy. I'm impressed." I had a bottle in my trunk, but just the usual stuff.

He shrugged. "We're classy people."

"I'm going to grab a snack," Carla said.

"Hungry?" Jordie asked me. He put the bottle down on his desk.

"Nah. I had dinner. You guys go ahead." I pointed at the PlayStation. "I'll get some thumb exercise."

"Come on down if you change your mind."

"I will."

I figured it would be OK with Jordie if I had a sip. There was plenty for the concert. It burned my throat, but in a good way. I had another sip to numb the burn. Then just one more tiny little drop, to push the numbness up to my brain.

I could hear them in the kitchen downstairs.

One more sip. There was plenty. Actually, I could drink a third of the bottle. That would be my share. I'd just enjoy it now instead of later.

Man, it felt warm in there. But good.

Carla didn't drink much. She wouldn't need a whole third.

This was nice stuff. The world spun a bit. I took a drink to steady things.

Wow. Real nice. I was feeling no pain. Me and Jordie. Going to a concert. Awesome. And Carla. Hot Carla. I took a drink to wash away indecent thoughts.

Damn. It was warm in there.

Another little sip.

Kinda dizzy.

Small sip.

Warm.

Sip.

Up. Side. Down.

What . . . ?

I was hanging. Dangling. Something pressing my chest.

Shoulder belt.

My hand found the buckle.

What?

Click. I twisted, felt a door latch.

Dark out. Where?

Crawled. Tried to stand. Threw up.

Sat down. My car—upside down. Smashed windshield.

Jordie! I got to my feet. Looked in the car. Nothing. Stumbled to the water, six feet away. Saw a shirt. Jordie's. Half on the bank. Floating. I stepped into the water. Felt around. Nothing.

"Help!" I got back on land. Looked at the car.

Oh, Christ—a body. Legs and a torso, sticking out from under the roof.

I rushed over. Saw. Puked again, my stomach kicking out acid, and then spewing emptiness. Her body was ripped open, nearly torn in half. Guts spilled. Carla.

I staggered away, clawed up the wall of the gorge to the road. "Help!"

"Shhh!"

I spun, fell.

"Quiet, man."

One of the homeless. In the shadows. Wool cap pulled low. Shaggy beard. One eye dead white. Gaps in his teeth. He limped toward me, his clothes smelling like rot, carrying a garbage bag full of empties. *Please, let this be a nightmare.*

He leaned over and put a hand on my arm. "Saw you roll the car, kid. Tough luck." He pointed down into the gorge. "I ain't no fan of the cops. They catch you now, it's over. DWI. Homicide. All over. Jail for a long, long time. Unless you're smart."

17

"What do I do?"

He let go of my arm and turned his hand palm up. "Advice ain't free."

I gave him all the money I had in my wallet. "Help me."

"Get home. Sober up. It's your only chance. Wait until morning. Longer, if it's still in your system."

"But how can I explain . . . ?"

"Trauma. You're in shock. You walked away from the accident in a daze. You don't remember anything."

"My friends . . ."

"Too late for them. They're dead."

They're dead.

Feeling dead myself, I stumbled toward home, hiding whenever a car came down the road. The long walk was like another endless nightmare. As soon as I got to my room, I grabbed the vodka and unscrewed the cap. My hands shook so hard, the vodka splashed out of the opening. I'd lifted the bottle halfway to my lips when I froze.

Sober up.

I had to wait. Be sober when the cops came. I took a burning hot shower, trying to wash the vomit and horror from my body and mind. I went to bed, curled up, and wondered whether it was possible to will yourself to die.

I kept hearing Carla's voice. Seeing Jordie's face. They were so happy together.

Somehow, though I was sure I'd never sleep, I passed out.

I woke late and looked out the window. No cop car. My head throbbed. My mouth was so dry, I thought it would crack. I was dying for a drink. Just one. I picked up the bottle again. The smell made me throw up. Nothing came out but sorrow.

I needed to report the accident. I reached for the phone a hundred times. I reached for the bottle a thousand times.

Jordie. Carla.

Evening came. I skipped dinner. Mom stuck her head in my room and asked where my car was. I lied. Told her I'd dropped it off for an oil change and they had to keep it until Monday. God, I wanted a drink. The bottle called to every cell in my body.

Life would be so much better with one drink.

But my life was over. I was as dead as Jordie and Carla. I deserved to rot in jail. Or die.

Where were the cops?

Tomorrow I'd turn myself in. I owed that much to Jordie.

I couldn't sleep. I fell into numbness, wracked with tremors. The night passed as I imagined their bodies decomposing in the gorge.

I was awakened by a knock on my bedroom door. I checked the clock. It was just after eleven a.m. I guess I'd finally fallen asleep.

The door opened. I sat up.

They came in. Jordie. Carla. Ghosts. But not.

My muscles went slack.

Todd stepped into view behind them. "First day's the hardest," he said. He sat down on the bed next to me. "You doing OK?"

I pointed to Jordie. "How? I killed you. Both of you."

"Hollywood magic, my friend," Todd said. He pulled some money out of his shirt pocket and tossed it on the bed. "I guess I made a pretty convincing homeless guy."

I stared down at the money I'd handed him last night, trying to piece everything together. "My car?"

"Still at my place," Jordie said.

"How? It was wrecked."

"Nope. Your Civic is right where you left it. We towed a wreck from the yard to the gorge."

I looked at Carla. "But I saw . . ."

"Cow guts," she said, making a face. "My uncle's a butcher."

"You doing OK?" Todd asked again.

"Yeah. No." I looked for a third answer, somewhere in between, but all that came out was a weak, wordless cry. I grabbed Todd, my body shaking, all the pain, all the fear, spilling out like soda gushing from a shaken bottle. I couldn't stop the sobs that jerked my body.

Other arms cradled me. "It's OK," Jordie said. "There's help. There's all sorts of help."

"I'm so sorry."

"Hush," Carla whispered.

I looked at her through blurred eyes. "You covered yourself with cow guts."

She nodded.

"For me."

"You're Jordie's friend."

"Am I?" I looked over at him.

He nodded, too. "But I think I might be your worst enemy for a while," he said. "From what I hear, it's going to be a bitch."

"It can't be worse than Friday night," I said. I thought about the wrecked cars at Jordie's place, and the wrecked lives of the homeless men who hung out by the liquor store. What would people give for a second chance? Or a real friend? I didn't know. But I was going to find out.

ABOUT THE AUTHOR AND THE STORY

Readers familiar with David Lubar's short stories and novels are likely surprised when they read "Here's to Good Friends," expecting lots of laughs and some weird events. Of course there is some humor in this story, and the climax is pretty horrifying. But if you want more humor and weirdness, you will find plenty in *Invasion of the Road Weenies* and *In the Land of the Lawn Weenies*, as well as in *Flip*, *Wizards of the Game*, *Punished!*, and *Sleeping Freshmen Never Lie*. That last novel was an American Library Association

David Lubar

Best Book for Young Adults, a New York Public Library Book for the Teen Age, a *VOYA* Top Shelf Fiction for Middle School Readers selection, and winner of the Michigan Thumbs Up! Award. *Hidden Talents,* the intriguing story of a group of boys in a special school for troubled and troublesome kids, was named, among other honors, an ALA Best Book for Young Adults and a YALSA Popular Paperback for Young Adults as well as an ALA Quick Pick. And *Dunk,* his most honored novel, was named a YALSA Popular Paperback for Young Adults, a New York Public Library Book for the Teen Age, and a Bank Street College Best Children's Book of the Year; it was also a One Book New Jersey Selection and winner of a Keystone State Reading Association Young Adult Book Award. His newest novel for young adults is called *Big Stink.*

A resident of Pennsylvania, David Lubar is always attracted to writing challenges, in this case the challenge of telling a story from the viewpoint of a chronic drinker. He says, "As a member of society, I was drawn by the feeling that there are a lot of kids out there who aren't getting the help they need." Studies suggest that there are more than three million teenagers addicted to alcohol in the United States, while several million more teens have serious drinking problems. According to the National Institute on Alcohol Abuse and Alcoholism, teens who drink before the age of fifteen are four to five times more likely to become addicted to alcohol than those who don't drink until they are twenty-one or older. Not only does drinking have a negative effect on memory and academic achievement, as it does for Brad, but drinking is also the leading factor in automobile deaths among fifteen- to twenty-four-year-olds.

The most effective way for a teenager to deal with his or her drinking problem is through a self-help support group, like Alcoholics Anonymous (AA). Friends and family of drinkers can get help from Al-Anon and Alateen at *www.al-anon.alateen.org* or 1-888-4AL-ANON (425-2666). Other sources of help include the National Drug and Alcohol Treatment Referral Routing Service at 1-800-662-HELP (4357) and the National Clearinghouse for Alcohol and Drug Information at 1-800-729-6686.

Plagued with eeps, jerks, and twitches, Alex
just wants to be treated like a normal kid.

Tic and Shout

GAIL GILES

"Mr. Donleavy, Ms. Baskin needs Cat to help with Alex.
He's, like, barking and snapping at people."

I looked up my from my trig test to see Lisa Higgins
standing in the doorway.

Surely there were a couple of hearing-impaired people
south of the equator or in a hole in the Arctic somewhere
that didn't hear her, but everyone in my class did.

"Barking? Don't go, Cat. He'll chase you up a tree."

"That's quite enough, Mr. Larkin. Prove your quick
wit on your test, please." Mr. Donleavy seemed as
amused with Doug as I was. "Catherine, bring me your

test. You understand, I'll have to give you a different makeup?"

You just betcha I did. I was halfway through a mind-cracking exam, and now I'd have to take another one. Yes, I got it: I'd seen the whole test, so it wasn't fair that I could look up how to work the problems, but I knew how to do the ones we had, and now I had to take my chances on a whole new test. Why?

Because Alex, my younger brother, was barking and snapping at people in his reading class. My baby brother was blessed with our genetic gift of Tourette's syndrome.

When I got to the freshman wing and rounded the corner of the hall where Alex's class was held, I heard the banging. Alex was body-slamming himself into the lockers. Ms. Baskin was trying to keep him from doing too much damage.

"Cat, thank goodness. He—I don't know—he just went wild in the class, and the other little cretins started barking back at him and howling, so I brought him out here and he suddenly started doing this. I know the other students stressed him, but I didn't shout at him or . . ."

"I know, Ms. Baskin." I eased behind Alex when he stepped forward, and when he slammed back, I pushed my knees into the back of his; he collapsed into me, and we slid down the wall, with Alex more or less in my lap. I took his hands in mine and wrapped both our arms around him and rocked.

"You didn't do anything, Ms. B." Alex relaxed a little.

"Some Tourette's, well—I know Alex can do it sometimes—he'll switch one kind of outburst behavior for another." Alex rocked his head back against me. Tired. I'd known when he'd been tired this morning that he hadn't slept well and that he'd be having a bad day.

"The only way I know to explain Tourette's," I continued, "is if you had a sudden urge to laugh at a funeral—really got a case of the ha-ha's, you know? If you couldn't stop yourself from laughing, and the more you laughed, the worse it got—I think that's what it's like for Alex and his tics."

"Don't talk about me like I'm not here," Alex said.

"Can I let you go?"

"I wish you—" His shoulder twitched twice. "Shit." He looked to Ms. Baskin. "That's not Tourette's; that's cussing."

I eased Alex off my lap. "You're too big for this. Can I finish the explanation or would you like to take over?"

"You. I'm tired. Got a headache, too. Those lockers are"—he twitched again—"hard."

When I looked over, Ms. Baskin was sitting on the floor with us. "OK, the funeral," I said. "If you want to keep from laughing at the funeral, you might do something like dig your fingernails into your palms. I think that's what Alex does when he bangs himself around."

"I know I should keep stress low for you, Alex," Ms. Baskin said, "but this was much worse than your usual tics. What can I do to help you?"

Alex rubbed his forehead. "Ms. Baskin, it's like someone opened my head and stirred with a stick. You're doing all you can do."

He looked at me. "New meds?"

"Maybe. Think you're OK for a while?"

"Who knows? Might be barking again by noon."

Ms. Baskin's classroom door burst open and two boys poured out, tangled in a flailing, punching, screaming heap.

"Shit," Ms. Baskin said. "Sorry."

"Tourette's," we said together. It was an old joke.

"The worst thing is — the world thinks *they* are the normal ones," Ms. Baskin said, getting up and nodding toward the two boys. "I'm not going to break it up because I don't like either one of you!" she shouted at the two combatants. They stopped immediately.

"That's not right," the bigger one whined.

"True, but if you had really wanted to fight, you'd have kept it inside. You wanted me to break it up," Ms. Baskin said. "Get up. Get inside." She raised her voice. "And anyone not in their seats when I get inside this door gets written up for provoking the fight."

I turned to Alex. "I'd have barked at them, too."

We stood. "Mom'll go ballistic, you know."

"I know," he breathed. When Alex wasn't ticcing, he was still as pond water. "She's already got the forms for home school filled out. And Dad said that if I want to handle high school, I have to handle her. He's not going to help."

The brawlers stormed out of Ms. Baskin's room, pink disciplinary slips clutched in their still-clenched fists.

"Dog Dude, this is all your fault. Your barking got us in this trouble." The smaller of the two said nothing but jabbed the air with his third finger.

"And you don't think home school might be better than this?" I said. "You just have to put up with Dad and me at home. I know Mom is too smothery, but she means well. C'mon, we're not as bad as those guys."

"The world is full of those guys. I have to learn to deal or else spend my life hiding behind Mommy."

The bell rang. "Eep, eep, eep." Alex jerked and squeaked like a terrified mouse. The bell had startled him. A stress rush and a plague of tics. It was going to be a long day, and I was sure both the principal and the nurse would be calling our mother before the day was over.

I went to Mr. Donleavy during my lunch break to see when I could take the makeup. Mr. Donleavy had his planning period then and was grading papers. "Come in, Catherine. Ms. Baskin sent me an e-mail about your situation. It appears this is something out of your control and out of your brother's. Alex seems to think you are penalized because of his difficulties."

"No, sir. Alex is the only one who suffers here. This is old news."

Mr. Donleavy knit his brows and kind of rolled his index finger indicating I should expand. "Sir, Alex has been showing symptoms of Tourette's for years. When I was much younger, I thought everybody's little brother acted like that. Then I got the picture that Alex was different, and I was embarrassed. And then I got angry that I was stuck with him. And then it all passed. He's a sweet kid. I can pretend I don't know him or I can help him. I was part of making the decision about him coming to a public high school."

"Isn't he a heavy load?"

"I can carry it."

"Well, I'm offering you a deal today. Decided before I show you your graded test. You can turn in the test as complete. You did about half. That means you did less than the other students but you'll be graded twice as hard on what you did. Or I can give you an entirely new test tomorrow after school."

OK. I felt pretty good about what I had done — but double or nothing, more or less? "I'll take the test as it stands."

"Good choice. Ninety-two. Congratulations."

By the time I met up with Alex after school, he appeared exhausted. He dumped his books into the backseat of the car and slid into the front like a slow-leaking balloon.

"What's the damage?" I asked.

"Math teacher put me and my desk outside for our test because I was 'eeping' and no one else could concentrate. Principal was doing a walk-by." He clicked himself into the seat belt.

"Crap," I said. "Did he—"

"Oh, he called Mom. From his cell. He knew about the barking because of the butt-munches that had the fight."

"I figure you shouldn't call them that when you make your case to Mom."

Alex's foot jerked forward and smacked the dash. Again. He grabbed his knee and held it. The foot kept jerking, so his whole body twitched. "Last time I thought I broke a toe."

Alex went still when the tic was over, and we didn't talk until we turned into our driveway. Mom was already standing in the doorway, waiting.

"I hate this part," Alex said, his face so utterly sad that it hit me. How long had it been since I had seen Alex smile?

Mom's overprotectiveness pushed Alex into a tic outburst. "I hear you had a bad day, sweetie," Mom crooned. She tried to put her arms around him.

Alex's whole body jolted and jerked. His arms flailed. "Sweetie. Sweetie. Fart. Sweetie. Fart."

Mom pulled away, and Alex lurched and shuddered down the hall and into the safety of his room. "Fart. Sweetie. Fart."

Mom sighed and headed for the kitchen. And now for the fallout.

"He's checking out of school as soon as I send the papers in and get them approved. I'm homeschooling him and that's final."

"Mom, he doesn't want that."

Mom put her hands on the edge of the sink and stared out the window. "I can't watch him suffer. I can't do it. Not anymore."

"You don't watch him suffer, Mom. I do. I watch it. And he's handling it. He wants to handle it. Don't smother him."

She whirled on me. Tears in her eyes. Angry, hurt, and something I couldn't name. "You can't know what this feels like. Smothering? That school is taking him apart piece by piece. I see him come home worse every day. You are not his mother. You can't—"

"And you're not his sister. You aren't there. He's tougher than you think. Don't crush him, Mom. Don't do it. He might forgive you for it, but I won't."

I left the kitchen. Alex was right. I hated this part. He couldn't get through this kind of stress. The tics wouldn't allow it. So I had to do it for him. I hated hurting Mom, but it had to be done. And everyone lost. Mom was already on antidepressants, and I was thinking about raiding her stash.

* * *

Alex was already in Ms. Baskin's room when I got there after school.

"Thanks for coming, Cat. I know you tire of getting these notes in your classes, but I've been thinking—"

"Mom called her," Alex said.

"Indeed, she did."

"Alex doesn't want to be homeschooled," I said.

"And I don't think he needs to be." Ms. Baskin came around her desk and sat in one of the student chairs near us.

"Can you and Alex give me a quick trip through his educational background? I got a flyby visit from the special needs director during our prep days before school opened. She didn't have Alex's file, but she told me I'd have a student with Tourette's syndrome, try to keep stress low as possible, and call if I had questions. She has about two hundred cases in her workload."

I sighed, scratched my eyebrow, then ran my fingers through my hair. "Alex wasn't diagnosed until late elementary school. First they thought he was ADD and hyperactive and I don't know what else. I was young, too."

"I got yelled at a lot and put out of class," Alex said.

"Then there was another doctor in Houston, and Alex was out of public school and in a private one in Houston for other kids with Tourette's."

"We looked like a bunch of clocks all going off at different times, but there was no yelling," Alex said.

"Then Mom homeschooled him. And then he went

to a self-contained class with an aide of his own for seventh and eighth grade."

"Why doesn't he have an aide here?" Ms. Baskin asked.

"Now, that's a great idea," Alex put in. "Dog Boy and his keeper. I'd really fit in that way. He could walk me on a leash. Give me treats when I didn't pee on the classroom floor." Alex shrugged. "Sorry, Ms. B. I get a little bitter." He waggled his eyebrows. "And sometimes I'm a little biter."

I groaned.

"Now, if you are going to be mainstreamed," I continued, "there's a committee that evaluates the student, and it decided Alex didn't merit a full-time aide. And Alex didn't want one. Why you didn't get your contact materials beats me."

"They should catch up with me by second semester or so," Ms. Baskin said. "And that's why the other students don't know Alex or understand his outbursts?"

"Right," I said.

"I've been kept in the closet," Alex said. "No, that would be wrong. Under wraps. I'm the mystery man. That's better."

Ms. Baskin stood and paced around the room. Her arms were folded across her stomach, and her forefinger tapped her opposite wrist in a rapid tattoo. Did she know she did it? Was it a tic?

She stopped and faced us.

"I think Alex could ease his stress if his classmates

understood what happens to him. Maybe we could get your mother and even the principal to see that Alex can handle being in school. I have an idea. I don't know how risky it is, but . . . it made so much sense to me when you gave the funeral example. Couldn't Alex explain to his whole class the same way? But instead of talking, you could do it with media? Freshmen are so MTV. Show them some examples, instead of telling."

"Are you talking about an assembly of the freshman class with Alex? . . ."

Ms. Baskin nodded.

"There's no possible way," I said.

"Yes, there is," Alex said. "There's plenty of possible ways."

"Alex, think. The stress. You couldn't handle it. You'd—"

"Have to have lots of help. Talk to the doc about some extra meds maybe. Rehearse the whole thing to feel secure. It won't be just me on the stage—there will be all the multimedia stuff. And besides, having a tic outburst will just be part of the show, right?" He looked at Ms. Baskin. "Right?"

She grinned at Alex. "I'll clear it with the powers that be. Here's a list of some materials I can get easily; you decide on the kind of media clips you want to run on the screens. I'll get the date set, the equipment, the people to run it, and all the permissions. You can tell me what else I need to do."

I rubbed my face with my hands. "Alex?"

"How big a disaster can it be?" he asked. "I'm already known as Mad Dog."

And I was Mad Dog's Cat. Disasters have a way of sweeping up the people next to you.

Alex and I decided on the film clips. I enlisted a few friends sympathetic to the cause, then I had to use outside sources. I went to the local news station, and they showed me how to capture a few clips when I explained, and even gave me ideas for a few more. Good ideas. Next, I went to the video store. I rented a stack of DVDs that were all on the list. Then I headed for one of the gigaheads from school.

"That's, like, pirating."

"It will be used once, no one is paying, and it's for a good cause. The question is, can you do it?"

"Easy-peasy, but it's like—"

"Illegal," I said. "I'm aware. I'll swear I did it. No money will be changing hands here. It's for a good cause. I'd write for permissions but I don't have time."

"I never did this," Gigahead said as he started working.

That night I got my camcorder and went to my best friend's house, then a football game, and to a party after. My brother had Tourette's, but *I* was obviously out of my mind.

*   *   *

It took three weeks to put together. Alex had been to his doctor. His adjusted meds had been a good thing. Tics were less frequent, of shorter duration, and not as . . . wild. More eeping, less snapping.

We had to work like the CIA around Mom. "Need-to-know info," we kept telling her. Now *she* developed a tic every time we said it. But we got the slides and photos and clips in order. I took them to Gigahead and he put them on one DVD, and then it was in the hands of the equipment guru.

It was the day. We had asked Mom and Dad to attend. The entire freshman class was filing into the school auditorium. Before I took my seat, I went backstage to see how Alex was handling it.

Alex looked good. Red shirt. Why try to hide? He'd be the only one on the stage.

"You sure you can handle this?" I asked him.

"Does it matter?" Alex said. He grinned. "I'm cool. This might be easier than walking into my first class in high school. At least now I get to explain."

Ms. Baskin walked toward us. "OK, Alex. The principal finally caved. No introductions, like you asked. He hates it, but he'll live. We let the kids sit a minute, then we bring the sound up and it's your show." She smiled. "Deep breaths. You're going to be a star." She turned to me. "Two minutes. Get your butt in a chair."

"We're a bad influence on her," Alex said.

"No kidding." I gave him a light punch on the arm and headed for the audience.

We sat in the dim light. I saw the equipment guru flip a switch and a loud, recorded voice shouted, "Hey, Spaz!" Then from another speaker came, "It's the Twitcher." "Jerk-Off." "Mouse Fart." "Dog Dude." "Woof, Woof!" "Don't bite me, Barker!"

The curtains opened, and a spotlight hit Alex, standing behind and white-knuckling the sides of a tall, old-fashioned wooden podium. Three screens filled the stage to his left.

"Hi, I'm Alex. I'm also known as Spaz, Twitcher, Jerk-Off, Mouse Fart, Dog Dude, Woof, and Barker." Alex twitched then. A head, shoulder, eep jerk. Then he took a deep breath. "There are probably a lot of names you call me that I haven't heard, but I would just as soon you keep those to yourself."

There was a small, uneasy ripple of laughter in the audience.

"But if you insist on calling me something besides Alex, Mouse Fart is my favorite."

The laughter was a little stronger.

"But, I want to tell you about me. I understand why you define me by my oddness. That's all you know. I want you to know more."

The ripple turned to squirming. This is where it might go south.

"I have Tourette's syndrome. It's not a disease. You can't get it from me. Not by standing close to me. Not by drinking out of my Coke. And be warned: your teachers have been told that you can't catch Tourette's. So if you watch too much TV and think Tourettes cuss uncontrollably, your teacher will be writing you up when you try it out on her after this assembly. Sorry 'bout that.

"Tourette's is a gift of DNA. I can only give it to my children. By sharing my DNA with someone. And since one of my tics is to shout 'You're fat!' when I see a good-looking girl, I doubt my DNA will be getting shared. Ever."

This time they laughed fully.

A hand shot up in the audience. One of our plants. "Great, a question."

My boyfriend's younger sister stood up. "Why would you do that? Tell a girl she's fat?"

Alex twitched and jerked and eeped. And eeped. And eeped. Then stopped.

"The smart people, like doctors and researchers, don't know, but Tourettes seem to blurt out something that is forbidden, what we shouldn't say, what would be the worst thing *to* say. It doesn't mean it's a true statement." He twitched again. Stopped.

"Something in a Tourette's person goes for the gold."

They didn't laugh big, but they smiled and chuckled. Were they seeing Alex as something more than his tics and quirks?

"Tourette's shows itself as physical reactions called tics that don't seem necessary or socially acceptable. I can't control them. It's kind of a brain fart."

Small laughter.

"Some of you have these tics in small ways."

The three screens filled with white light. The old song "People Are Strange" played in the background.

The first was a clip that took forever to make. It showed my boyfriend sitting on a couch. A close-up of his face.

Alex spoke. "If you or anyone is in a social setting and is embarrassed, you will have a physical reaction that you can't control—the same way that I can't control my eeping or twitching." Suddenly Brian's face flooded with color. Starting at the neck, he flushed red, turning darker as the color rose to his hairline.

"You call it a blush. And you can't stop it, make it go away, or make it ease off. It's going to happen. If you had Tourette's, that would be a tic."

We had to show Brian pictures of naked women in front of his parents to get him to blush like that. His father might still be laughing.

And there was some laughing in the audience, but it was the "I've been there" kind.

"Now," Alex said, "here are some reflexive tics. They happen without thinking, but the ticcers could stop them if they wanted. But since the tics are socially acceptable, they don't."

The second screen filled with a party scene. A '70s disco song filled with *umm*s and *uhh*s backed up the action. My best friend saw a good-looking boy walk into a room, and in a heartbeat she tossed her hair, tucked down her chin, and looked up at him through her eyelashes. There was a slight shift in her torso that pushed her breasts forward, too.

"The flip-tuck-thrust mating-call tic," Alex said. Isabel, my friend, stood in the audience and spread her arms, then air-kissed the audience.

They applauded. Not many seemed to see Alex jerking and batting his head with one fist.

Isabel did and kept up her act for a minute until he calmed himself.

The third screen came up: the football game. Loud, pounding, headbanger music. Players pounding their own chests, growling and woofing, knocking their helmets together, picking their knees up high and running in place in a mad attempt to release nervousness and stress.

"This is acceptable on the field. As is this."

Screen one pulled Brian's red face into a dot and filled in with a pro baseball team. We'd had a jazz band guy write a short, jazzy lament that said, "I just don't know what to do with myself." We looped it to play over and over as the players adjusted their crotches endlessly, scratched their butts, and spat on the ground, while the catcher and the plate coaches fanned their fingers in front of their faces like startled birds and the pitcher didn't seem to know what to do with his cap and he fingered and refingered the bill.

"In its setting, that's normal behavior. I've done all of that; well, I don't spit, really. I don't spit, and I've kept my hands off my private parts, in public at least, since I was ten or so."

That one broke them up. The girls blushed and laughed. The guys just howled. Guys are so easy. Crotches and butts get 'em every time.

"But, I can't confine the banging and woofing and thumping to a field. I might do it in class, and that makes me a freak."

Low murmurs. Losing them, Alex.

"Now let me show you something that really looks like Tourette's."

All three screens filled at once. One showed a famous drummer, grimacing and twitching as he pounded. Another, a guitarist and singer, so famous for his twitching, quirky, jerking rendition of songs that he stood next to a comedian who had become famous for his parody of the singer and they sang, jolting and spasming together. On the third, young people danced in a club, looking as if they had stuck their fingers in a live socket for the duration of the song.

The screens went back to small dots of light and then to blank.

"So this is the deal. I don't want much. I'm not that different. You guys have done everything I do. Well, maybe you don't often make a noise like you're torturing mice." Alex eeped and jerked. "That was fake, by the way, a demonstration. But you've done most of the other things I've just shown you. The big difference is, blush aside, you can control it. I can't.

"If you are around when I have a tic outburst, the best thing to do is ignore it." He looked over the audience. "Seriously, that takes the stress off. Either keep talking, or say nothing, or walk away. Just ignore it and I have a better chance of calming down. I will never *be* one of you guys. I'm not asking you for that. But I'd like to stay here. Just to be around. To watch the real world, to see how it works. I'm just asking you to ignore me so I can."

All three screens filled with the message IF YOU WANT TO LEARN MORE ABOUT TOURETTE'S SYNDROME, GO TO: www.tsa-usa.org.

Scattered clapping broke out, but it wasn't much. The principal stood by the door. "Thanks, Alex. You may all return to your classes."

I headed for the steps to the stage. Alex was coming down. "So how bad was it?" he asked.

"You were great," I said. "You even ad-libbed a little."

"Alex, I'm proud of you, son." Dad shook Alex's hand.

Mom stood next to Dad and nodded to Alex but said nothing. She was eavesdropping on the departing audience.

I was, too. It was a little too easy to hear the "woof,

woofs" that came from several spots. Snippets of conversation that included ". . . guy's a freak," "Sure, he's cute, but . . . ," ". . . actually, like, snaps his teeth at people?"

They were still talking *about* Alex, not *to* him.

"Oh, Alex," Mom said, her eyes filling with tears.

"Mom, they're doing what I asked them to do. Ignoring me."

But the next day Alex had a tic outburst and began repeating the last words his teacher said over and over again. Mr. Davis asked Alex to step outside until he calmed down.

"You don't have to do that, Mr. D.," Kyle Michaels said. "He's not bothering anybody, and he'll chill in a minute. We're cool with it."

In gym a hulking senior asked Alex if he could get a driver's license.

"Nope," Alex said.

"'Cause of that jerking thing. My little brother told me you, like, eep out."

"Nope, because I'm fourteen. I have to be sixteen to get a license."

"That eeping thing make you a smart-ass?"

"Nope, I have to work on that," Alex told him.

The interesting thing was that Alex told us the stories over dinner. We never talked about Tourette's with Alex. We'd ignore it around him. Then Dad and Mom would quiz me about Alex's day. Things were changing. I felt curiously left out. Dad smiled at Alex as he talked, but Mom didn't and neither did I.

I looked at Mom's face and realized she was totally concerned with Alex's disease; Dad was only interested in Alex's handling of it. Where did I stand? I looked at Alex. No ticcing, speaking confidently. I knew where I wanted to be.

Alex, not me, asked Mom not to send the home-schooling papers in. She agreed to wait until the end of the quarter to make a decision. I could see how much she hated it. And I saw how much she needed Alex to need her. How long had Alex known that?

Three days later the phone rang at nine o'clock in the evening. For Alex. It was a female. A young female.

I watched my phone until I saw the connection had ended before I burst into Alex's room.

"Who, what, when, where, and how?"

"I'll tell if you don't write it up for the newspaper," Alex said. He was eeping and jerking like a string puppet handled by a convulsive. "Summer Thames asked me to go to the dance after the football game Friday. She said she knew I'd never ask her."

"Oh, my God," I said.

"Are you behind this?"

"I wouldn't do that to you."

Alex shivered. "I didn't think so. She thinks I'm cute. She said so."

"You are cute."

"That's so true," Alex said.

I sat on his bed. "This is huge."

"She said that if I say she's fat, she'll say I'm ugly, and we'll be even."

I smiled. "The girl has style."

"Go away," Alex said. "I have to die of happiness now."

I don't know how the football game went. I worried about Alex and his date the whole time. I couldn't see them in the stands. I couldn't hear barking and I didn't see anyone running away pointing and screaming about a biting student, so I guess most of Alex's worst tics were in control.

Brian and I went to the dance, and Alex and Summer were already there with a knot of other freshmen. All skinny as spring colts. Girls giggling and boys posturing, uncomfortable in their new teenage selves. Alex was ticing a lot, but mostly shoulder twitches that were controlled. The band played and the dancers were scattered.

"I'm going to go talk to Alex," I said.

"Don't," Brian said. "Let him do this. You'll smother him."

I turned to Brian and stared. "Smother him?"

"Could happen," he said.

I looked back at Alex. And stayed where I was.

The lead singer finished his song, then stepped back and spoke with his band members. He strode to his microphone and grabbed it. "Hey there, we had a request called in a coupla days ago. This is an oldie and the request is for some special lyric substitutions. So listen up and have some fun with this one."

I saw Summer and her friends light up with excitement. She pulled Alex to the dance floor as several couples surrounded them. The band kicked in the music and the singer urged his baby to shake it, and then he leaned in close and sang the new lyrics to the familiar old tune: "Tic and Shout!"

Summer and her friends all jerked and twitched in unison, and eeped. At first, Alex just looked at them, confused. Was he the butt of a cruel joke or . . . then Summer grabbed Alex's forearms, pulled him to her, and planted a full-on kiss right on his lips.

Alex started eeping and jerking and twitching. I don't know if he was dancing or ticcing. But he looked just like everyone else. He was one of them.

This was probably a charity gig for Summer and her friends. Who knew? Alex might return to being Dog Dude by Monday, or he might have a couple of weeks of friends before they tired of him. Or maybe not. Maybe these kids would give themselves a chance to find the Alex I knew.

All I was certain of was that right now, and for the first time in longer than I could remember, Alex had a big wide smile on his face.

ABOUT THE AUTHOR AND THE STORY

Gail Giles is the author of five distinguished and disturbing novels for adolescent readers: *Right Behind You; Shattering Glass; Dead Girls Don't Write Letters; Playing in Traffic;* and *What Happened to Cass McBride?* In *Right Behind You,* a fourteen-year-old boy tries to start a new life after his release from a juvenile detention center where he was put away for murder. In *Shattering Glass,* a high school boy is murdered by his classmates because they hated him. In *Dead Girls Don't Write Letters,* the narrator's supposedly dead sister shows up at the family's home and it's difficult to tell what's real and what's not. In *Playing in Traffic,* an ordinary high school boy with a rather dull life gets involved with a pierced and tattooed Goth girl who provides more excitement than he ever imagined. And in *What Happened to Cass McBride?* a disturbed young man whose brother has committed suicide blames Cass McBride and buries her alive in a coffinlike box. Among many awards, Giles's novels have been nominated for various state book awards and selected as Book Sense 76 Choices, American Library Association Quick Picks, and New York Public Library Books for the Teen Age.

Gail Giles

Born and raised in Texas, Gail Giles was a remedial reading teacher before she turned to writing full-time. During her teaching years, she says, she had a student with Tourette's and so did a lot of research in order to better understand and help him. It was that student who first described the feeling of being a person with Tourette's that Alex states in the story: "It's like somebody stirred my brain with a stick."

To research further for this story, Giles says she went to the website that Alex recommends in the story and then followed the links on that site as well as on other sites and was happy to find "that most of the medical gurus agree on the ways to live with juvenile Tourette's. Some disagree on types of or even the need for medication, but that happens in every disease of the nervous system." What the Internet resources provided most were the types of tics and symptoms, and their percentage of likelihood of presentation, which she was able to incorporate into her story. "I certainly wanted to disabuse the TV and movie notion that the cursing symptom is the most common of all tics," she says. "I also wanted to show that there can be some control if the affected person can be in a reduced stress situation."

Life is worse than a gigantic headache for Amy.
And sympathy is not what she needs.

Triclops

JULIE ANNE PETERS

The mask fit snugly over our heads. It smelled like sweaty rubber. Skull said, "Maybe if we hugged each other?"

"Don't touch me," Keiran snapped. Her arms crossed her chest defensively.

Inside the rubber mask, our voices amplified. I said, "Let's try standing back to back." The silk drape was loose, at least. We all turned and scuttled into place.

My eye, the red eye, picked up the rising sun and glowed. I gripped the plastic eyeball, the handle we'd glued on, and twisted. The eye rolled and bobbed.

"On three," Keiran said. "One, two . . ."

We each took a step in opposite directions. And stalled.

Keiran said, "We're total morons. Amy, you lead."

Lead. OK. "To the right. My right." I sidestepped. It was hard to see through the tiny peepholes under my eyeball, and the dim morning light didn't help, but finally for the first time ever, we were moving as a unit.

Skull said, "Let's undulate." He bent his knees and dipped.

Keiran went, "Stop it. We're not squid." She elbowed him. We shuffled another foot. "Are all the eyeballs working?" Keiran asked.

"Check," I said.

"Mate," Skull said.

Keiran exhaled wearily. "Skull. Sound effects."

With my back to Skull, I couldn't see the recorder, but I felt him reach into the pocket of his Jams. Without warning, King Kong shattered the morning. A scream and a deep, resounding bellow about punctured my eardrums.

Skull undulated, and to keep our heads in the mask, Keiran and I had to copy. "Cool it," she yelled. I felt her kick him.

The second sound—a rabid, enraged Godzilla— exploded my brain. Skull amped up the volume. Keiran said something I missed, then *CRASH!* A car wreck: tires squealing and people shrieking.

"What was that?" Keiran shouted.

Keiran or Skull's ankle hooked mine and I tripped. We veered to the left, twisted and weaved, and I sped up, the grass sloping, our momentum carrying us to the pool area. Screeching brakes and crunching metal, horns blasting, people squalling, a cacophony of sounds mixed over roars and growls. We tumbled, out of control, and I lurched, took a header, and crunched to the ground. A body smothered me, then another, and my cheekbone smashed against my eyeball.

Inside the mask, there was heavy breathing. Skull asked, "Is everyone OK?"

I was the first one to start laughing. Skull giggled like a monkey. Even Keiran rumbled in her chest.

A guy from a second-floor apartment hollered, "Do you know what time it is? Shut it down or I'm calling the cops."

I couldn't stop laughing. Skull clamped a hand over my mouth, his shoulders still shaking. Keiran wriggled out of the costume, wrestling Skull and me free.

Keiran said, "You added a car crash to the sound track? You asstard." She shoved Skull.

He grinned at me. "Authentic, yes?"

I had to smile. "Since we're crashing a Halloween party? I guess."

Keiran muttered a curse. "We'll have to do better tonight. We don't want to look like . . ." She let the thought dangle.

Skull finished it for her, "The geeks we are?"

Keiran went, "Whatever."

Mom had already left for work when I dropped the costume off upstairs. Keiran, Skull, and I walked to school. Well, Keiran and I walked. Skull rode his skateboard.

"We're going to be so cool," Keiran said. "I can't believe it's finally here."

"Me neither." The Halloween party was that night, Friday. The three of us had been working on our costume since the beginning of summer. Drawing it, scanning and photoshopping on Keiran's PC, buying fabric and foam, carving molds, pouring latex. Painting, airbrushing, anchoring the eyeballs. We'd attached the heads and sewn the drape, painted the eyes bloodshot, engineered a way for them to move. Three eyes. One head. Each eye rotating in its socket independent of the others so that it looked so totally freaky-weird people were going to scream. Especially when we cranked up the sound effects.

We still had one problem — the triclops tripping over its own six feet.

When we bombed the party, though, Melanie Grayson was going to freak. Out. I couldn't wait.

Keiran had come up with the idea for the triclops. A three-eyed monster. Skull found out when and where the party was going down at Grayson's. We weren't invited, of course. Melanie Grayson would never invite a bunch of

geeks to her X-treme Halloween party. A triclops was crashing the major party of the year. Woot. Monster invasion.

"We'll have to dress in the bushes when we get there,"
Keiran said as we rounded the corner into the quad.

"No." Skull rolled up on his board. "We should dress
at Amy's. We can trick-or-treat on the way to the party."

Keiran huffed. "Get real. This isn't kindergarten."

Skull flipped his board to catch it right in front of
Keiran's face. "Reality is an abstract concept, an illusion,
which cannot be gotten or achieved."

"Was I talking to you?" Keiran turned to me. "Was I
talking to him?"

I didn't have to answer. This was Keiran and Skull,
always at it. "Take a shower and wear deodorant," Keiran
ordered Skull. "Ames and I are not dying of your toxic BO
under that rubber head."

Skull said, "Eat my Altoids."

I laughed.

Keiran slit her eyes at me. "Don't encourage him."

How did I get so lucky? I wondered again. I couldn't
believe the three of us were friends. Or still friends after all
the times I'd let them down—

No. I couldn't think about that. I had to live in the
moment.

We had nothing in common, really, besides the geek-
iness factor. Besides the fact none of us made friends easily. I shouldn't speak for Skull and Keiran. I was the one
who didn't do friends.

Skull only scared people because of his shaved head and piercings.

Underneath he was the sweetest guy ever. Skull and Keiran and I met that day in the school clinic when Skull blew a backside twist in the quad and split his head open. He had hair then. Black and curly. He'd stood at the sink examining his gash in the mirror. He'd had to lean over the sink to see it, since the lights were out. Keiran was scrunched on a chair in the corner, sulking or something. She'd stormed in a few minutes earlier and snarled, "Don't talk to me."

Not a problem, I'd thought. I just wanted to curl up and die.

Not die. I wouldn't die. The sickness I had wouldn't kill me. I was more afraid of death than life. What if I took the sickness with me when I died?

Skull had been fingering his cut, and I couldn't hold it in anymore. I staggered to my feet and hurled in the sink.

Skull went, "Dude."

I felt him behind me waving the air. Coughing and gagging.

Keiran muttered, "Gross."

I'd stuttered a few deep breaths, scooping water into my mouth to rinse. I hated when people were there. When they saw. A hand tickled the back of my neck. "When's it due?"

My pulsating head lifted. What? The word came out, "Wha?"

Skull pointed to my stomach.

I didn't get it.

Then I did.

"No," I'd managed to say. "I'm jus . . . sick."

Keiran's eyes met mine in the mirror, and I saw a flicker of something. Sympathy? I didn't need sympathy. I needed Roo. Roo was the thing I needed to find, the place I needed to go for help.

"Don't worry, darling," Skull had said, taking my hand. "We'll raise our child together."

"God," Keiran mumbled. "Blow chunks on him."

The warning bell rang and I hustled to my locker. Why'd I ever schedule algebra first hour? Keiran was still ragging on Skull, now about being the Go Eye. The green eye. He wanted to be Yield Eye. During the design phase, we'd decided to add color to the three-eyed theme. Red for stop. Green for go. Yellow for yield. No one would get it but us.

"Amy, we'll meet at your apartment at eight," Skull called, his voice carrying over the din in the hallway. "Good luck on your test."

Keiran shouted, "Ames. Easy A."

My stomach knotted. I was ready for this midterm. I was. I'd studied hard. I was good in math, but still, I got nervous before a big test.

The halls cleared and I took the stairs two at a time. Veering down the C wing, I twitched at the pang.

No. It was phantom. Fear. Anxiety.

The lights seemed especially bright. Were they always this glaring? The hall was long. I didn't remember the hallway curving and widening like this.

I was queasy.

No. This couldn't be happening. Not now. Ten minutes ago I felt euphoric. High. I was psyched about Halloween.

I should've known it wasn't real. Invincibility was a warning. *I'm coming for you,* it said. *You forgot. I'm always here, lurking. You can't feel good. You're not allowed to feel good.*

The classroom door at the end of the hall quivered, like a mirage. Bleary heat waves roiled my stomach. I should've taken a pill. I might have time. I reached into the front pocket of my backpack and discovered my little plastic case was missing. The one I could never be without. I checked the finger pocket on my jeans. Empty. Where was it? I must've left my pills at home. In my rush to rehearse this morning, to be ready for tonight.

I was cratering. I had an algebra midterm. *Not now. Please,* I prayed. My backpack was lead. I hugged it to my side as I stumbled into class. Distorted faces swelled and shrank. People's bodies swayed like sea grass. Mr. Ochoa said something, but the words didn't register in my consciousness.

I had to throw up.

I forced my feet to move, to find the second aisle. I dragged, tripped, and gouged my hip into the edge of an empty desk. The desk legs scraped across the floor, sounding like squealing brakes at a stoplight. I winced and slipped into my seat.

Mr. Ochoa passed out the test, and I thought, *I'm going to pass out. I'm freezing. I feel dizzy.*

I had to concentrate. I had to. Equations swam before my eyes. The lights reflected so brightly off the paper I thought I was going blind.

Pain. If I could hold back the pain, I could make it through. *Please, please let me through.*

I didn't remember retrieving my pencil. I was deep into calculating equations when a claw of pain ripped through my right eye. The scritch of pencils around me sounded like a million ants digging out a colony. I was on page two, almost at the end. Three more problems.

I wasn't going to make it. I had to hurl.

Mr. Ochoa raised his head from the papers he was grading. He frowned at me. I handed him my test.

"I'm sick." I heard my disembodied voice. "I have to go."

I didn't wait for him to say it. I knew the rule: No makeup tests.

All my teachers' voices from the past filled the echo chamber of my head. "You're sick again?" "You can't leave now." "You've lost too much time." "Automatic zero." "You're failing, Amy. Failing."

Failing, failing, failing. I heard it every time I liked a teacher. I hated letting them down.

Home. I had to get home to Roo.

Vomit first. I almost plowed into a person exiting the restroom as I charged in. It was Melanie Grayson.

No. I wouldn't cry. I'd cry later, when it was over. The party. After I missed another major event in my life.

I disconnect. I have to. I become two people: Well Amy and Sick Amy.

Sick Amy has a name for the dark. *Roo.* She doesn't have a name for what happens in the dark. Roo holds her, shields her; Roo hides her in a blanket of black and deep and warm. Roo tries to make it better. Roo tries.

White. WHITE. Roo can't fight the white. Roo tries. Sick Amy begs Roo, *Please don't let white in. Don't let it stay. Kill it.* Roo clashes with white, but white always wins.

White is pain. White is agony.

Her mom hangs a black-out curtain in Sick Amy's room at the apartment. The curtain conjures up Roo. She's grateful Roo is here. She loves her mom.

Relax, she hears the voice. The soothing voice on the recorder. Sick Amy tries to listen, to obey. She slackens her jaw, her arms, her eyelids, forehead. She repeats the chant from the biofeedback lessons. "My arms are heavy and warm. Warmth is flowing in." White won't release. It squeezes, cuts, rips; it wrenches her right eye out of her face. White stabs, reams, ruts.

She has to vomit. She has to hurl.

She can't get up. She can't unglue herself from the Roo grave where she's lain for a lifetime, for an hour, an eternity. Where she wants to join with Roo.

Dizziness. Queasiness.

She slides a wooden leg off the bed and lifts her head.

Scree. Screeding yeddow whiii. She can't move her mouth to make hard consonants now. The slightest movement jars. Her nose runs. She has a cold. Cold symptoms.

She plods her clubfeet to the toilet. She barely makes it, and heaves. Her stomach opens and her throat releases the vomit. It gushes out into the water and splashes her face.

Mom is there. "Oh, honey," she says. "Sweetie." Mom holds her by the forehead. Cool hand. Amy leans into her mom's hand and lets her hold her up. "Did you take your medicine?" Mom asks.

"Yeh," Amy whimpers. It hurts to talk. "Is nah working."

"Honey."

Mom hugs her, but it hurts. Excruciating pain. She doesn't want her mom now. She doesn't want people around her. Go away.

Relief. For a moment. Better. Dizzy, but the white is yellow, yellow-green. Roo beckons; Roo welcomes.

Sickness, fever, hot, cold. She lowers to the bed and onto her side, jamming her sick eye into her palm. Her Roo. She hears her tinny voice go "Roooo." Draw down the darkness, she thinks. Blacken the white.

Mom's hand on her back feels like a knife in her spine. Fracturing her vertebrae; the pounding in her forehead with a hammer to her eye. Stop. Go away.

The soft cool of the bed folds in on her. Her Roo. Roo finds her pillow. She burrows her right temple into the Roo of her pillow, her black warm soft dark Roo.

"Do we need to go to the emergency room?" Mom asks. Her roaring, screaming voice in Sick Amy's ears. Strident sounds. Mom sits on the bed.

No! Don't! The motion is turbulent ocean, sea, sinking ship, throwing her from side to side, crashing against the railing, throwing up.

Still is best. Still and quiet Roo.

"Amy?"

"I fiiiine."

It's too expensive. Every time it costs like five hundred dollars. Her mom can't pay it; she doesn't have the money. She can't get insurance anymore. This new job, the apartment. Please, Mom, go away.

"Keiran called. She wanted to come over early to practice."

Amy presses her head into the pillow. *Make her go away. Please, Roo.*

"I told her you had a migraine."

Tears well in Amy's eyes. *Keiran hates me,* she thinks. *She has to hate me. Skull. They hate me. They should. I miss everything. I can't have friends. I have sickness. I need Roo.*

"She said to feel better. She'd call you later."

Later. Better. When would better come? Never. She has to believe it will come, that there's an end to the suffering. The torture. To the fear of never feeling better.

Mom stands up and the bed, the boat, rocks and roils. White, spearing, crushing blows, stabbing spears forever.

"I wish there was something I could do for you."

Leave, Amy thinks. *Go away. I don't want you here. Don't cry. Please. Don't care so much.*

In fifth grade, Sick Amy missed sixty-eight days of school. They wanted to hold her back, but Mom said no.

Well Amy compensated. She made up the work. On good days, great days, she worked three times as hard. She was smart. She'd get ahead. She wouldn't fail. She couldn't fail. Her mom, her teachers.

In sixth grade, Sick Amy missed eighty-four days. She changed schools so they wouldn't know. In the new school she could find her way to the nurse's office blindfolded, without vision or hearing or touch. Don't touch. Her head knew the feel of the cold leather cot, the crease in the headrest, the scratchy wool blanket. No Roo at this school. She'd ask; she'd beg, "Could you turn out the light?" The mean nurse, the lump of human flesh and garbage, would say, "I can't do my work in the dark. Do you want to call your mom again?"

No. No, she didn't want to call her mom again. Not twice in one week. The ringing phone exploded in her eardrums, the flashing lights made her dizzy, her head pulsed. "Mom?" Her tinny, tiny voice.

"Oh, Amy." The disappointment in Mom's voice. "Again?"

"Can you come and get me?"

The slight hesitation. Her mother's sigh. "I'll be there as soon as I can." She failed her mother. She failed everyone.

Middle school. The nurse who understood, who had migraines, too. She knew to turn out the lights, to cover Amy with warm, soft blankets. To create Roo. A cold washcloth on her forehead, or an ice pack, alternated with the hot millet bag. Amy loved the millet bag. She could smell the grain being microwaved, inhale it up her nose. Soothing smell, like cereal. Fragrant Roo relief.

For a moment, for a while. Relief. Then white burned through, bored through the heat and cold; the sickness seeped back in.

The worst part, besides endless suffering and sickness, was the hopelessness. The powerlessness of knowing it would come for her and there was nothing Well Amy could do to outrun it. The medicine helped; it staved off the white. But she had to remember to take it right away, when the euphoria, the excellent feelings, lifted her high and gave her hope. At a time when there was no such thing as pain or hurt or suffering, Sick Amy had to remember that wasn't her world.

It was cruel, almost. She could never allow herself to feel too good for too long.

Then the letdown always came. Letting everyone down. All she ever did was let her mom down. Her teachers. Friends. She didn't cultivate friends because who needed a friend they could never count on?

Amy couldn't even say the *M* word. *Migraine.* Because saying it, verbalizing it, thinking it, might summon the white. Might trip the light. She couldn't think about it and she couldn't not think about it. See? Cruel.

The day Skull and Keiran appeared, Sick Amy was in the throes of a long, bad, major migraine that would turn out to be a three-day torture session, ending in the emergency room with a melting shot of morphine.

She saw Skull the next week, after she got back. After she'd recovered from her hangover. The aftershock. When you're in that much pain for that long, it takes a while for your body to recover. Skull had stitches. She didn't know his name then. He'd shaved his head. He saw her in the hall and waved at her. He said, "Have you decided on a name for our baby? I was thinking Vomitra."

Amy had laughed. He'd caught up with her. He started walking with her. Skull, she found out later. He'd named himself, or renamed himself. He was in the process of remaking himself, he said, because he liked a girl. Amy knew who. Keiran.

What could she say about Keiran? Keiran ruled her galaxy. She was a celestial body in motion. Skull and Amy were her moons.

I extended my legs as far as they'd go on the outdoor chaise and wondered. I wondered again why Skull and Keiran stayed friends with me. They were so in love with each other, they didn't need me.

My toes curled, and I willed blood to every extremity of my body. My muscles ached, my skin was sensitive, and my ears rang. The aftershock. I was drowsy. Completely relaxed. My stomach was finally settled. Mom made me eat a cup of soup and crackers. It tasted amazing.

Everything was amazing after. Life. Living. Wanting to live forever. All my senses were hyperreceptive.

Touch especially. Feel. Heat. The sun beating on my face. I craved light after forty-nine hours of darkness.

A *whump* beside me made me flinch. "I hate you," Keiran said.

I swallowed hard.

Keiran clicked her tongue and cast me a withering look. "Not about that. At least you had an excuse."

What was she talking about? You never knew with Keiran.

Keiran kicked off her purple Crocs and sprawled on the chaise next to me. The pool at the apartment complex had been emptied for the winter, and the aqua paint on the concrete was peeling. Since we were here Friday morning, practicing our triclops tango, someone had left a naked doll baby in the middle of the pool. Face down. Friday seemed so long ago.

I didn't want to know, yet I did. "How was the party?" I asked.

Keiran reached into her purse and pulled out her shades. She slipped them on. "I don't know. I didn't go."

"What?" I lifted my head. A streak of white ripped through my right eye, but it was OK. Phantom pain. Aftershock. I tugged my knit cap down over my ears. "Why? You guys could've found someone else to be the third eye."

Keiran made a sound in her throat, like, *Please.* She said, "You're red. You're Stop Eye. No one else can do red eye like you."

I studied Keiran. She'd cut her hair. When? Streaked it, too. In the sun, it was every color of the rainbow. She was so cool. Too cool for me. What did she see in me?

"Stop looking at me," Keiran said. "I know I'm a freak."

I closed my eyes and turned away. The sun was healing. Hot.

"I just didn't want to go without you. It wouldn't have

been any fun. Besides, we're a team, you know? We're tri-clops."

"You would've been alone with him inside what's basically a giant sleeping bag," I said. "You idiot. Did you even think of that?"

Keiran said, "I don't like him that way."

I muttered under my breath, "Liar."

Keiran twisted her head. "I don't."

She sounded serious. I fixed on Keiran's face. "*He* does. He loves you."

Keiran blinked. "He told you that?"

Some things didn't need to be said out loud.

Keiran added, "If he likes me, that's a problem."

I didn't get it. Why Keiran wouldn't let him in. Why she wouldn't let herself be loved.

Then it hit me. Maybe we had more in common than I thought.

"He's pissed as hell," she said. "He'll probably never talk to either of us again. That's the good news."

The gate to the pool area screaked open. Keiran and I nearly crunched heads as we spun to see who was coming. "Speaking of devil spawn," Keiran mumbled.

Skull tromped across the cement. He stopped behind us, his shadow elongating on the chaises. He said, "You are dead to me."

Keiran went, "Move. You're blocking our sun."

I pivoted my head slowly, gently on my sore neck to look up at Skull. "I'm sorry," I told him.

"Not you," he said. "Don't be sorry. You couldn't help it. *You* could." He drilled a finger into Keiran's head.

She swatted him away.

He clomped around her chaise and plopped at the edge of the pool. His long, lean legs dangled off the side. He set his board beside him. Third appendage.

"So did you go?" Keiran asked.

"I went. You think I want to deprive Melanie Grayson of her special time with me?"

I tried to suppress a laugh.

"Don't encourage him," Keiran said. "So how was it?"

Skull rolled his board behind his head and rested his elbows on it. "Bunch of amateurs. Our costume was off the hook."

"Our costume kicked," Keiran said.

"It was beast," I went. "Literally."

We were quiet. The calm wrapped around us. I closed my eyes and breathed in the joy of relief. Keiran let out an audible sigh. "I didn't want to go, anyway. It never was about the stupid party."

"Yeah," Skull said.

"Liars." They were just trying to make me feel better.

"Was it for you?" Keiran asked. Skull swiveled his head to stare at me, too.

Was it about the party?

Wasn't it?

I admitted, "I would've liked to go." Same way I would've liked to go to Keiran's poetry slam last month.

Or Skull's boarding exhibition. My own birthday party. I couldn't remember the last birthday I hadn't spent in bed with a migraine.

Skull yelled, "Oh my God!" He scrambled to his feet and, poised like a diver, jumped into the empty pool.

"What the . . . ?" Keiran scooted to sit up. So did I.

Skull hollered, "Hang on. I'm coming."

Keiran lowered her shades and frowned at me. I shrugged.

Skull's head popped up at the edge of the pool. He was breathing hard as his arm extended into the air. "She's OK. She's still alive." He was holding the doll baby.

He scrabbled over the side and pretended to catch his breath. Clutching the baby to his stomach, he gasped. "Vomitra. I told you to wear your arm floaties."

Keiran leveled a look at me. "If you want him, he's yours."

I thought, *Right. You know you love him.*

Skull skated over to me and set the doll gingerly on my chest. "Oh, darling," he said, dropping to his knees. "There was no need for that." He took my hand. "I told you we'd raise her together."

I cracked up. It felt good to laugh, to let it out. Or in.

Skull motioned to Keiran, like, come over here. She sighed heavily, but got up. Skull said, "Group hug."

We snaked arms around one another. We pressed our heads together. I went, "We'd have been an awesome triclops."

"We still are," Keiran replied.

"And baby makes four," Skull said.

"Shut up." Keiran smacked him on the head. "You're such a spaz."

I took Keiran's hand, then Skull's. I squeezed. "I love you guys." I never thought I'd say that. Believe it for real. Life's too short not to let people in.

"Ditto," Skull said quietly.

"You know I'm not into emo," Keiran said. She flopped onto her chaise and reached into her purse. She retrieved her sketchbook. "Here, I want you guys to look at this. It's an idea I had for next year's costume." She flipped open the cover and paged forward. She held up a drawing. "Melanie Grayson was my muse."

Skull's eyes waffled. My eyebrows arched. Skull said what I was thinking. "Are those . . . bra cups?"

Keiran smirked. "Genius, right? I'm thinking we'll call ourselves the 3-Ds."

ABOUT THE AUTHOR AND THE STORY

A resident of Lakewood, Colorado, Julie Anne Peters is the author of sixteen books for young adults and children. Her first young adult novel, *Define "Normal,"* won the California Young Reader Medal, the Oklahoma Sequoyah Book Award, and the Maryland

Black-Eyed Susan Award, all voted on by young readers as their favorite book of the year. It was also named a Best Book for Young Adults by the American Library Association and, at the time of this writing, was being produced as a musical for the Lifetime channel. *Luna,* Peters's novel about a transgender teen beginning her transition from male to female, was a National Book Award Finalist. Her other works for young adults include *By the Time You Read This, I'll Be Dead; Rage: a Love Story; Between Mom and Jo; Far from Xanadu; Keeping You a Secret;* and a collection of short stories called *grl2grl.*

Julie Anne Peters knows about migraines firsthand, having suffered from them for most of her life. She says that "a migraine is more than a headache. The pain of a migraine may be so intense that a person will not be able to move, think, or function at all." Although the pain of a migraine centers on the eyes, forehead, or temples, other symptoms include nausea, vomiting, dizziness, depression, sleepiness, congestion, sore muscles, and sensitivity to light, sound, and strong odors. A migraine can last anywhere from two to forty-eight hours or longer, if left untreated.

It's estimated that as many as 10 percent of children are "migraineurs" and even more teenagers suffer from the condition. The exact cause of migraines is unknown, but Peters's research indicates that factors that trigger episodes include flickering lights, changing weather patterns, perfumes, anxiety, tension, foods such as cheeses, nuts, hot fresh bread, chocolate, caffeine, and pizza, and chemical additives and dyes. Because stress is a confirmed migraine trigger, teen migraineurs are particularly vulnerable to heavy school workloads, excessive extracurricular activities, unsettled routines, and difficult or challenging relationships with friends, family, or teachers. Over time, the burden of migraines may cause serious depression and personality changes.

"One of my worst migraine memories," Peters says, "was the time my mother planned a 'Sweet Sixteen' surprise party for me. She invited all my friends, our extended family, and neighbors. When I walked in the door, everyone yelled, 'Surprise!' and I threw up. I'm still mad I spent my 'Sweet Sixteen' in bed with a migraine."

Fortunately, Peters notes, "recent medical breakthroughs are vastly improving the lives of people living with migraines. Lifestyle changes, biofeedback, and natural remedies are alternative treatment options."

Although he knows better,
Eddie just can't stop himself.

Under Control

CHRIS CRUTCHER

School isn't exactly my strong suit. My name is Eddie Proffit, which when they separate you out because you can't keep up, not only puts you in Special Ed, it *makes* you Special Ed. That's where they tried to stick me in grade school, and they got away with it for a while until the school janitor, Mr. Bartholomew, who was my best friend's dad, figured out I was smart off-the-charts and rigged up ways to keep me focused long enough to show the teachers I didn't need to finger paint four hours a day. Mr. Bartholomew's son, Billy, and I were best friends until the day Billy got killed when four pieces of Sheetrock fell on him from behind and snapped his neck, which was only three weeks after my dad expired after forgetting to let the air out of a truck tire he was fixing before prying off the lock ring, which exploded and about ripped his head right off his body. That all happened the summer before my freshman year in high school. You think I wasn't good at school before, you should have seen me *that* year. Every time I'd close my eyes to get away from some teacher who was trying to bore me into a coma, I'd see dead people, and they were the people I loved most. That was three years ago. I'm better now.

I was missing a dad, and Billy's dad was missing a son, so we hooked up to take the edge off and that's worked out pretty well, all things considered. When I get in a pinch that needs a man's touch, I call him. He's not the janitor at our school anymore, because he came down on the side of intellectual freedom when the administration banned a book that a bunch of the "academically unfocused" kids, which included me, liked a lot. Imagine that; a guy gets fired for giving kids who don't read a book they want to read. The administration said it wasn't the janitor's job to make policy decisions and sent him packing. Now he's the janitor at the public library, where he gets to help make policy decisions because they understand how stories touch lives.

My core problem, the thing that made my elementary teachers and my mom think I was destined to be a greeter at Wal-Mart or a Waffle House manager, is my short attention span. Man, people with short attention spans say I have a short attention span. A journalism student who's doing a student profile on each of the graduating seniors for our school newspaper asked me what I thought I'd remember most about high school. Without hesitation I said, "The clock." There's a Seth Thomas mounted just above the exit in each and every classroom. It's wood with Roman numerals and a little pendulum behind glass just below the face. The pendulum moves but the hands don't. I swear I can be sitting in a class, praying for the creator of the universe to please, oh please, let it end before I have to yawn so loud the teacher thinks a bear is roaring, and the hands not only stand still, sometimes they go backward. Being trapped in a high school classroom gives me hope that I may live forever.

So I have to do things sometimes that, you know, keep my head in the game. That often means trouble. The problem with a short attention span is that when your focus slips away from what your teacher or your mother thinks you should be thinking about, it doesn't disappear, it jumps to something else. I can be "staying on task," listening to a teacher, and he or she will say a word that catches my fancy and off I go. Like the other day when Mr. Harrison, my U.S. government and civics teacher, was talking about the "situation" in Iraq and how if more young men weren't willing to make the sacrifice for their country, we might have to go to a draft. Within seconds I was thinking I felt one, then about writing a first one, and by the time he asked me a question, I was visualizing a bartender drawing one in a pub, and that's how I answered his question about a draft.

Mr. Harrison and I have a running war because he doesn't "believe" in ADD. He also doesn't believe in depression or in eating, conduct, or anxiety disorders, all of which he causes. The summer after my sophomore year, the Bear Creek Sawmill closed down, and by the time school started my junior year, our town's population was cut in half, as was the population of our school. A lot of good, young, progressive teachers lost their jobs, and a lot of tired, old, conservative teachers stayed because they had seniority. I don't want to sound ageist but I'm seventeen, and when faced with the choice of excited young teachers and tired old when-I-was-your-age teachers, well. . . . OK, I'm ageist.

The point is, Harrison stayed and Ms. McDonnell didn't, and so we have a right-wing Christian conservative government/civics teacher who, if you were truly going to stick to the idea of "separation of church and state," you'd have to cut him in half. Now I may be a little ADD but I'm interested in learning as much as I can about the world, because, as they usually say at graduation, I'm about to inherit it. From what I see in the news, I've got my work cut out for me.

I should say one more thing about ADD—which means I'll probably say five or six—and that is that what a lot of people don't understand, particularly people who don't *believe* in ADD, is that just because I bounce off a subject prematurely, which pretty much means before my teacher is ready for me to stop thinking about it, if it's worth much, I'll get back to it. You ever see a little kid's *really* messy room? If you're a good parent or big brother or whatever, you want them to learn to clean that place up. But what looks like a messy room is, for kids like me, a whole bunch of *projects*. You do one for a while and then you do another and another and another, and then you move back to one of the old ones, and if left to your own devices, you'll deal with all of them in due time. It is not a good idea to make a kid like that clean up his unfinished projects, because he might just have a temper tantrum, or worse, get even. Leave him alone and in the end you'll have a whole bunch of projects finished.

Close your eyes and picture that room. That's what it looks like inside my head. One way to keep me focused on one of those projects longer than I normally would is to add *heat*. Intensity. I learned that early, and one thing Mr. Bartholomew (who I call Bart, at his behest) taught me a long time ago was that when teachers got on my back about not paying attention, I needed to add enough intensity to the situation to make it worth paying attention to. Great survival skill. Getting the pattern? See the train wreck coming?

The intensity source comes ready-made, because during my freshman year I got into that aforementioned censorship battle with Mr. Tarter, our English teacher, and also the Very Reverend down at the very fundamental, very Red Brick church. I've said Harrison is kind of hard-core conservative, but Tarter made him look like Ted Kennedy. Tarter thought church and state were the same outfit. At any rate, the censorship issue came right on the heels of the deaths of my father and my best friend, and I was running with a hard-core nothing-to-lose attitude, and before it was over, the book was banned and I had said some very unchristian-like things about a lot of Christians, most of whom didn't deserve it. Four years later, Harrison can still quote me word for word, and often does. I'm calmer these days, but I can quote myself word for word, too, and often do. It doesn't take much to drive up the intensity in civics to the point where I have no problem attending. God, I love a good fight.

Harrison's disadvantage in a classroom squabble with me is that he's stuck with linear, rational, cause-and-effect thinking, which I guess has a lot to be said for it. What he doesn't understand about ADD folks, particularly smart ones, is that we think in metaphor a whole lot of the time, so one thing reminds us of something else and we have no problem bouncing over to that something else without filling in the blanks. We score really high on the How-Is-This-Thing-Like-That-Other-Thing test, if we can hang in there long enough to get that far. In other words, Harrison walks; I fly. Fast. He loves to call me out about the censorship issue because he thinks he can crank me up beyond reason and then tell me I'm being unreasonable.

He backs up that assertion with the fact that I was thrown in the psych unit in the heat of the book banning battle. But that was only because I went to the church that housed the people challenging the book and did some fast talking that may have indicated to some of them that I was crazy. I would have talked slower, but they were chasing me. Oh yeah, and I may have intimated I might be Jesus. All it was, really, was ADD on adrenaline. Not crazy.

Eye of the beholder, huh?

What Harrison and Tarter never really understood, I think, was that back then I wasn't so much against banning books—I didn't yet understand the harm that can do—as I was struck by the issues in the book they wanted banned. The characters included a gay teacher, who Tarter and Harrison didn't think should exist anywhere in the world—certainly not in the land of the free where the homos are getting too brave—and a bunch of characters of different races and a girl who had been sexually abused and a man who had molested a girl—different girl—and several kids on drugs. I think about the only things the author left out were midget bowling and people who are aroused by their pets.

But it was tastefully done.

Tarter and Harrison and the rest of the Red Brickers mistook their success in banning the book for winning, even though the author was alerted and sent five brand-new, signed copies to the public library, and about half the kids in the student body either checked those out or ordered a copy off Amazon, and we carried them, front cover facing out, to our classrooms, the cafeteria, even to PE. When school officials tried to confiscate them (our personal property and the property of the county library), the library threatened a lawsuit and the rest of us went out and bought more copies, and the author, who isn't Stephen King, is probably still vacationing in Boca Raton.

But Harrison chalked it up as a win, and he loves to bait me in current events class because he remembers me as the "liberal who lost his butt" in the censorship battle of 2003. I didn't know a high school kid could be called a liberal *or* a conservative. I thought we were called sociopaths.

At any rate, I love it that Harrison thinks this way, because he always sets me up to set him up. A lot of the hottest debate surrounded the gay teacher character in the book, who, by the way, didn't do any gay things in the story. But he was a good guy, and the Red Brickers were pretty sure that would make us kids want to go out and get nekked with others of our same sex. Harrison still thinks gay marriage is a current event, even though in most places in the country no gays can get married because marriage is all sanctified and stuff. Harrison has decided that being gay is a choice, though he's never been able to explain to me why any kid would choose something that could get him beat up daily in high school or at least held up for relentless derision. So on Gay Marriage

Day we're in class discussing that topic and I decide to start things off slow by saying that anyone against gay marriage is a bigot. That thins out the people who were going to be on my side quite a bit, but you want to identify your friends early when the main point is to create intensity so you're not bored into a coma for most of the class.

"If we're going to have this discussion, Mr. Proffit, could we make it a reasonable one?"

I tell him that would be fine with me, then repeat my assertion.

Harrison decides it's not a good idea to play *Crossfire* in the classroom, even though there are at least ten kids simultaneously telling me what an ignorant jerk I am. He wants them to tell me I'm an ignorant jerk one at a time.

They do.

"You seem to be of a minority opinion, Mr. Proffit. Would you like to reconsider?"

In far less time than it takes to tell you, I am reminded of a situation where Abraham Lincoln had called his cabinet together for a policy discussion. Lincoln was famous for keeping people in his cabinet who disagreed with him so he consistently had a view of all sides of an issue. I can't remember this particular issue but it was big-time controversial, as issues can become in hard times, like say, a civil war, but when it came time for a vote, Lincoln said, "All those wishing to vote in the positive say 'Aye.'" His was the only *aye*. "All those wishing to vote in the negative say 'Nay,'" and all the cabinet members chimed in. Lincoln said, "The *ayes* have it." It doesn't take a majority to be right. With Abraham Lincoln by my side, I am undeterred.

"Nope," I say. "No reconsideration. A bigot is someone who is strongly partial to his or her own group, religion, race, or politics and is intolerant of those who differ."

Harrison says, "Good memory. How does that make someone who's against gay marriage a bigot?"

"Give me one argument against gay marriage or gay anything else that isn't religious," I say.

Harrison stares at me; I can see him searching.

"It's a biblical argument," I tell him. "Take the Bible out of it and there's no argument. I'm feeling strange; that's almost reasonable."

John Markee, a defensive guard on the football team and the guy who holds the county record for growing a potato that looks most like Richard Nixon, says, "It's filthy. That ain't biblical."

"It's also not a reason to make it against the law," I tell him. "Lots of filthy things are legal, starting with you naked in the locker room." Oops.

John gets up but so does Harrison, and John sits back down. I'm closer to the door than John, so there is an even chance I'll get out of this day alive because he is also a shot-putter and they have a track meet today. Pulverizing an ignorant jerk in the classroom gets you a three-day suspension. "About ten percent, conventional wisdom tells us, of every population is gay," I say. "That's two-point-three people right here in this room. Could I get the two ten-percenters to stand?"

Believe it or not, nobody stands. "There it is right there. If people weren't bigots, two people would be at attention right this minute. But it's the point-three I'm concerned with. You know . . . a little bit country, a little bit Barbra Streisand. John?"

John gets up again, faster this time. So does Harrison, but I sense he's getting tired of protecting me and might be slower next time. He tells me to be respectful.

"It's not disrespectful to call somebody point-three gay if you don't think there's anything wrong with being gay," I tell him. "But I get your point."

"You better get his point," Markee says, "or you're gonna get mine." He shows me his fist. It looks like a ham. I think of Christmas dinner, because that's how my mind works, and I see potatoes that don't look like Richard Nixon, and gravy and dressing and turkey, but the intensity I'm using to hold my focus shows me Christmas dinner covered with ketchup that is really my blood and suddenly I'm back.

"Who in here is against gay marriage?" I ask the class.

About half the hands go up, followed by two or three more in the wake of stern looks by friends.

"How many don't care one way or another?" Most of the rest of the hands go up.

"I won't ask how many are for it, to save you from Mr. Markee stalking you with his point-three percent."

Class is half over and my mind hasn't wandered once. I do believe I've found a cure. "So, just over half the class is made up of bigots, a bunch more are willing to let them be bigots, and a very few aren't."

It may surprise you to know that the half of the class I'm calling bigots don't like that very much and they begin calling me names and telling Mr. Harrison to make me sit down and shut the hell up. Harrison still thinks he can bring me around, though, because he beseeches them to take me on. They do, and they're beating me up pretty good, but I do a trick all ADD folks should learn, which is the broken record. When you've re-created the general chaos that is the inside of your brain in your immediate environment, find a simple thought and stick to it. I simply keep asking them to give me a line of reasoning against gay marriage that isn't religious, so I can take them off the bigot roll. Somebody says it's immoral and I ask who decides what's moral, and up pops Jesus and Leviticus, a pairing the real Jesus might seriously have cringed at. What these bozos don't get is the more the classroom looks like the inside of my head, the calmer I get. This intensity is intoxicating. I might just take a nap.

The word *bigot* is bouncing around in my brain creating all kinds of images, so I ask everyone to close their eyes and look ahead twenty years, but say that it's OK if

Harrison looks ahead only ten because I don't want him seeing himself in a walker. Surprisingly, no one is willing to close their eyes. There are some unruly kids in this classroom. Harrison should have better control.

"Well, then *pretend* your eyes are closed and you're looking ahead twenty years. Who wants to be George Wallace?"

"Who the hell is George Wallace?"

"Watch your language," Harrison says.

"Who the heck is George Wallace?"

I look at Harrison. "You want to tell them, or you want me to?"

"It's your funeral," he says.

"Google old George and the first picture you'll see is him standing at the gates of the University of Alabama in 1963 posturing to stop black students from entering that university," I say. "Bunch of people in Alabama thought he was the bravest, coolest governor they'd ever had. 'Course he didn't have the *huevos* to really stop 'em because he was nose to nose with the Attorney General of the United States, who had the National Guard at his disposal, should he need to dispose of George Wallace. Who wants to be Orval Faubus?"

Blank stares.

"Same song, second verse," I say. "Arkansas. Actually first verse. He got famous in 1957. All you gotta do is get yourself on CNN with your bigoted ideas about gay people and in ten to twenty years you can be a bigot in

Britannica just like Wallace and Faubus. It doesn't stop there. You'll be in the company of any number of good ol' white guys who decided Native Americans were taking up too much space, or who thought the Japanese should all go to concentration camps during World War II because they looked like the enemy even though they had been here as long as the people who sent them there, or you can hold hands with the corporate leaders who've always thought Mexicans oughta be able to come across the border to work for next to nothing and get no health care and then turn against them when it's politically correct to do so." I'm glad I'm a runner. I can say several long sentences in a row without breathing. When you breathe, other people might get a chance to talk, and my mouth is working about the same speed as my brain right now.

And I go for the kill. "So, Mr. Markee and the rest of you gridiron studs, have you figured out that on a team of twenty-two ball players, no pun intended, statistics say two of you, plus, are gay? What if you're the center? What if it's the quarterback? Down! Set! Oooops." And that's when Harrison loses total control of his classroom.

What I didn't consider was this. A cross-country runner can only outrun a football player if he has at least a hundred-yard lead.

"You want something for that eye?" Poppa Bartholo-mew asks as he drives me to my home. Only one eye is swollen shut. I could have driven my own car if they hadn't ice-picked my tires.

"Naw, by the time they let me back in, it'll be good as new."

"At the risk of telling you something you already know," he says, "civics is required; if you don't pass, you don't graduate. I was janitor at that school when Harrison was a student. He's pretty tightly wrapped. You might want to be a little careful what you say in his class."

I sit back in the seat, letting the sunlight through the side window soothe my wounds. "I know, but you know how my mind works, Bart. It doesn't have an editing function. Got an ace in the hole, though."

He says, "It better be the ace of spades."

"That it is, my good friend and mentor, that it is. You think Harrison wants me *back*?"

ABOUT THE AUTHOR AND THE STORY

Eddie Proffit's behaviors are quite typical of some teenagers who have ADD — attention deficit disorder — or ADHD, which includes hyperactivity. Though accurately diagnosing and treating this problem has been difficult, estimates are that between 3 and 5 percent of all children have this disorder, boys far more often than girls. These individuals tend to be impulsive, easily distracted, and have difficulty in following directions, completing tasks, planning ahead, and even sitting still for more than a few minutes.

If you have read Chris Crutcher's *The Sledding Hill,* you will have recognized Eddie Proffit in this story as that novel's hero. Eddie, as he says, is three years older in this story, though he's just as feisty, just as impulsive, and just as likely to get himself into trouble.

Besides writing *The Sledding Hill,* Chris Crutcher is the author of nine other novels—*Angry Management, Deadline, Running Loose, Stotan!, The Crazy Horse Electric Game, Chinese Handcuffs, Staying Fat for Sarah Byrnes, Ironman,* and *Whale Talk*—along with a book of short stories titled *Athletic Shorts,* and *King of the Mild Frontier: An Ill-Advised Autobiography.* Three of those books are considered among YALSA's 100 Best of the Best Books for Young Adults published during the last four decades of the twentieth century, while two others are among YALSA's 100 Best of the Best of the 21st Century, 1994–2003. His books have also received a Cuffie Award and a California Young Reader Medal and have been named among *VOYA's* Top Shelf Fiction for Middle School Readers, as well as being nominated for numerous state young adult book awards.

Crutcher is also the recipient of the Margaret A. Edwards Award for Lifetime Achievement from the American Library Association, the ALAN Award for Contributions to Young Adult Literature, the National Intellectual Freedom Award, the Writers Who Make a Difference Award, and the Celebration of Free Speech and Its Defenders Award.

Along with writing, Chris Crutcher has been a child and

family therapist focusing on abuse and domestic violence in Spokane, Washington. He says, however, "I'm not a specialist on attention deficit disorder, but there's a good chance I've had it all my life. Most of my junior high and high school life I felt dumb because it was so hard for me to pay attention and because I was so bored. My mind hopped from subject to subject because a certain word was said, or because something happened in the room that reminded me of something else, and off I'd go. I created Eddie in my image."

When you have the kind of disability Aston has,
there's only one way to handle it.

Way Too Cool

BRENDA WOODS

He was thirteen with smooth chocolate-colored skin, taller than most men, and as he often told anyone who would listen, way too cool.

It was the Friday before the start of Christmas break and he was looking forward to two weeks of freedom. He grinned as he opened the front door.

"Do you have your inhaler, Aston?" his mom called out from the kitchen. The same question came from her lips every morning. Every morning.

His grin vanished as he fingered the inhaler in his jacket pocket. "Yeah, I got it," he replied. He gave the screen door a gentle push, stepped outside, and headed to school.

Rosa Parks Middle School was a mile from his house, and unless someone gave him a ride, he walked.

"Take the bus," his pops advised when it was cold.

Aston replied, "The bus ain't cool."

His pops would sigh. "You have asthma."

Tell me something I don't know, Aston wanted to say.

His backpack was nearly empty, and he took long strides. The sun was shining, trying to warm the morning air, but it was useless. He pictured Nikki waiting for him on the school steps and hurried.

He was less than half a block from school when his chest got tight. He fumbled in his pocket for the inhaler and shook it. He put it to his mouth and was getting ready to take two puffs but decided not to. He was trying to wean himself. He stared at the gray plastic device. *If it weren't for this madness, I, Aston James, would be one of the coolest brothers on the planet,* he thought as he glanced toward the steps.

There she stood: Nikki. She had big green eyes, and her skin was the color of caramel candy.

He was popular with the honeys and he'd had a few crushes before, but this was more. He was still holding the inhaler when she reached for his hand.

"You have asthma?" she asked.

He glimpsed a hint of fear in her eyes and lied. "Naw.

I mean I used to but I grew out of it." How many times had people told him that? That he would grow out of it? How much more did he have to grow? Three inches or six? "Just an old inhaler I found in my pocket," he added as he wound up his arm like a major league baseball pitcher and threw the inhaler as far as he could. It sailed over the tops of nearly leafless trees and landed in the street.

"You sure you should do that?" sweet Nikki asked, her pink lip gloss glistening.

Aston slipped his hand into hers and smiled, "Ain't nuthin'."

He studied the place where his inhaler had fallen as the first bell rang, committing it to memory. Cars barreled down the street and he wondered if their wheels had already crushed it into the asphalt. He took a deep breath as the school doors closed behind him.

Nikki leaned her head into his shoulder. "My daddy said you could come over during vacation . . . but only in the daytime when my mom's at home. And my sister Yolie's comin' home from college, so you might get to meet her."

"Yolie. What kind of a name is that?"

"Short for Yolanda?"

"She as fine as you?"

"She ain't all that, but she thinks she is."

He laughed and led her to her homeroom.

"Hey, Nikki!" one of her girls, Carlita, yelled. Then she added, "Hey, Aston," and gave him a finger wave.

Aston, always cool, tipped his head to the side and flashed Carlita a smile. His teeth were white and perfect and he knew it.

The minute hand of the clock caught his eye as Nikki whispered, "See ya."

He rushed to his classroom, weaving through the hall between the lingerers, and slid into a desk just as the second bell rang.

His friend Ray nodded at him. "What up, dawg?"

The teacher, Mrs. Roberts, scanned the room like a watchdog, her eyes landing on Ray. She didn't allow talking. Aston smirked.

About a quarter of the seats were empty, and Mrs. Roberts shook her head as she rattled off the names. "This is a school day . . . a full school day," she interjected. "So you can tell your buddies who are missing in action that they will need notes from their parents on the first school day after vacation, or they will have detention." The watchdog fumed.

Eyes rolled as snickers and boos popped up all over the room. "Tell our buddies?" someone mocked.

"That will be enough," the teacher commanded.

Quiet came and Aston's mind began to drown out everything in the room. The teacher was still talking, but Aston no longer heard her as he proceeded to do one of the things he was best at, daydreaming.

Aston James pictured himself piloting a stealth aircraft. It was what he wanted more than anything. The Air

Force Academy. To be a pilot. To sail the skies. Ever since he could talk, airplanes and airports had fascinated him. "How do they stay in the air?" he'd asked his pops. "Can we go to the airport?" he'd begged his mom. Building model airplanes had become his hobby. By the time he was nine, Aston could identify every aircraft. By the time he was ten, he understood aerodynamics.

But asthma had robbed him of his dream, and he'd put the models away. Little kid stuff. His pops offered him alternatives: aircraft design, aerospace engineering. His mother told him she was praying for a small miracle, but so far her prayers hadn't been answered.

"It's not the worse thing. You can still play sports, and it's not like you have cancer or anything. Plus there are lots of people who have worse asthma than you," his baby sister, Kiley, had snidely remarked.

Kiley was almost right. Sports were cool and he could sink a three-pointer now and then. When he'd played little league ball, he'd hit more than his share of home runs. He could send a football through the air with precision. He could almost hit a golf ball as far as Tiger. He had all the skills. And with this new preventive medicine they'd come up with, he hardly ever had to use the nebulizer his mom had bought. In fact he hardly had to use his inhaler except when he had a cold or during the fall and winter or when something he was allergic to found its way into his nose. Kiley was right. Almost. The Air Force didn't take asthmatics.

"Aston?" The teacher startled him.

"Huh?"

She handed him his test paper.

A 98 percent along with a big red A was printed at the top, and Mrs. Roberts smiled at him. He folded it quickly before anyone could see. Aston James was way too cool to get A's, especially in math, pre-algebra to be exact.

Aston James coughed. His chest felt tight. The bell rang.

He was headed to the school office for his extra inhaler when Nikki slipped up beside him.

"Where you goin' in such a rush?" she asked.

He lied again. "Nowhere."

"Then walk with me to my class."

As they made their way through the noisy, crowded, locker-lined halls, Aston felt his chest getting tighter. He needed his inhaler. He needed it now.

"Why ain't you talkin'?" Nikki asked, trying hard to sound like she was straight out the ghetto.

"Just thinkin'."

"'Bout what?"

"'Bout what I'm gonna get you for Christmas."

"Just make sure it ain't too expensive, cuz my daddy will have himself a fit."

He wanted to tell her not to worry. It couldn't be too expensive because he only had ninety-seven dollars. Money he'd saved mostly from his birthday and twenty dollars that had come a few days ago with a card from his grandmother who lived in Georgia.

Nikki gazed up at him and smiled.

He forgot about the inhaler as he ushered her into her class.

Second period he spent doodling. The teacher was going on and on about World War II, and his mind turned again to aircraft. Aston drew a detailed picture of a P-51 Mustang, the best fighter plane of that war. Maybe his pops was right. Maybe he had a future in design or engineering. He smiled.

Before long, the clock had ticked away the forty minutes and the bell rang. He was barely out of the door when Nikki, surrounded by her little clique, greeted him. With a glance, she dismissed them and they bumped their way into the crowd, designer bags clutched to their sides. Girls were like bees, he thought, and Nikki was a queen.

They spent Nutrition making plans to see each other during the break. She would be practicing ice-skating, she told him. Would he come to the rink and watch? He hated the cold but said yes, picturing her in her little getup, twirling, practicing figure eights. She was kind of innocent and as sweet as candy. He squeezed her hand under the table, and her head rested on his shoulder.

Again, he walked her to her class. Then he darted. The day wasn't even half over and for the second time he made it to his classroom just as the bell rang. This having a girlfriend stuff was hard work.

The teacher was already talking.

Can't they give us a break? Aston thought. It was the day before a holiday, which was the same as a holiday in his mind. He muffled a cough with his hands.

"The human body is a mass of cells . . . specialized cells. And now it's movie time," the science teacher said as he flipped off the lights.

Cheers and hoots flew around the room until the movie started. It was about cell division. After five minutes, Aston was nodding, but the coughing kept him from falling asleep. His chest suddenly felt like someone had it in a vise. That was how an attack hit him sometimes, quick and without warning.

He slung his backpack over his shoulder and crept through the darkened room toward the back where the teacher was sitting. "I need to go to the office and get my inhaler," Aston whispered.

"You have asthma?" the teacher asked loudly.

Aston could see the partially lit faces of some of his classmates as they turned and stared. *Oh perfect,* he thought as he felt his armor of cool beginning to vanish.

"Yes," he replied between coughs.

The teacher slipped him a hall pass, and Aston skulked toward the door.

By the time he reached the office, he was panting. "I need my inhaler!" he gasped.

"Sit down," the office lady said as she rushed into the school nurse's office. "The school nurse is off," she added as she rummaged through the box of medications. "You're Aston, right?"

"Aston James."

"Here it is," she said as she pushed the box into his hand. She had that sorry look in her eyes. He hated that look.

"Thank you." He pulled the inhaler from the box, put it to his mouth, and squeezed. Nothing. He tried again. Still nothing. He shook it desperately. "It's empty!" he roared.

The office lady told him to relax.

How could he relax? "I can't breathe!" he told her. His coughs became more violent.

Just as the office lady turned on the PA, the principal walked through the door. "We have an emergency," the office lady told her.

"It's empty," Aston said. He felt defeated. He wasn't cool. He was a jackass. At least that's what his pops would say when he found out. All to impress a girl. Then, instantly, his mind shifted the blame to his mom. Why hadn't she checked the inhaler at school like she always did? That new job she had was taking up all of her time. This was all her fault.

Then he remembered.

He bolted from the office and sped like an escaping prisoner toward the school doors.

"Aston!" the principal yelled as she chased him down the hall. "Call 911!" she screamed to the office lady. "Now!" she added.

Aston butted through the door with his shoulder into the outside. Maybe it was still there. Maybe.

The principal called out, "Aston, stop!"

He didn't even turn around. Finally, he made it to the curb. His eyes darted around, searching. Fallen leaves peppered the street.

The principal reached him and placed her hand on his shoulder. She was out of breath. "Sit down. We called 911."

"It has to be here!" he gasped, coughing, his lungs shrinking, becoming smaller and smaller.

"What?" she asked.

"The inhaler."

"It's empty," she reminded him.

"Not that one—the one I threw away. It has to be here."

Her face said *why?* but she didn't ask as she helped him look.

In the distance, he heard the faint sound of a siren. Then, under a clump of leaves, he glimpsed a shred of familiar gray plastic. He hoped his eyes weren't playing tricks on him. No, there it was. He dove like a ballplayer toward a loose ball and found himself on his belly in the damp, cold street. He grabbed his little lifesaver and examined it briefly before he shook it and took one puff, then another. Instantly, his lungs began to soak up the air. He gazed up at the principal and smiled. Then she helped him, Aston James, Mr. Cool, up from the street and led him to the curb like a stray animal. Ten seconds later the paramedics arrived.

"What's the problem?" one of them asked.

Aston owned his malady, "Asthma." He held up his inhaler. "But I'm good now."

They put him in the back of the ambulance and examined him. "You're still a little tight," they informed him, then gave him a breathing treatment.

"Asthma is nothing to play with," another one remarked after talking to the principal. "People die."

I know, Aston thought. *I know. But I, Aston James, am way too cool to die.*

ABOUT THE AUTHOR AND THE STORY

Born in Cincinnati, Brenda Woods grew up in Los Angeles and continues to live there. She is the mother of two adult sons and recently became a grandmother.

When an English professor encouraged her to pursue a career in writing, she declined. Instead, she chose a career in the health sciences. With a BS degree in community health and a certificate in physical therapy, she has worked as a physical therapist for nearly twenty-eight years.

But she did write during her spare time, and her first short story was published in 1999. Her first novel, *The Red Rose Box,*

Brenda Woods

won a Coretta Scott King Honor in 2002. It also received the Judy
Lopez Memorial Award for Children's Literature and was a finalist
for PEN Center USA's 2003 Literary Award. Her second novel,
Emako Blue, about how a drive-by shooting affects the lives of five
Los Angeles teenagers, was an International Reading Association
Young Adults' Choice as well as an American Library Association
Quick Pick. Her newest book, *My Name Is Sally Little Song,* tells
the story of a young girl and her family who escape from slavery
in Georgia and seek protection with a group of Seminole Indians
in Florida. She says, "My goal as a writer is to allow children to
examine not only the past but the present as well. By doing this,
we allow them to impact the future in a positive and thoughtful
manner."

Woods's many years of public service, she says, prepared her to
be a writer who understands people. She particularly understands
asthma, because her younger son had his first asthma attack when
he was only two years old. She notes that trips to the hospital and
the doctor's office were frequent, he was hospitalized twice, and
that he missed many days of school. Current data suggest that
nearly twenty million Americans, including nine million kids
under the age of eighteen, have asthma. Every year more than five
thousand people die from the disease, and asthma rates continue
to rise worldwide.

Olivia may spend her days in a wheelchair,
but don't you dare call her handicapped.

Good Hands

RON KOERTGE

"Listen," says Brittany, "Kent called me last night."

Olivia looks up at her friend. "What's he doing calling you? He hasn't e-mailed me in a week."

Brittany shuffles the books she's carrying: red one on top, then in the middle, then back on top again. She has her mother's big hoop earrings on, and they're way out of proportion to her face. Her makeup is also over the top. Too much green and blue. If she had parakeets perched in those hoops, it might work. She could go on *American Idol* and be colorful.

"He started off talking about *The Scarlet Letter*," Brittany says, "then his band, and then he said he doesn't want to be your boyfriend anymore."

Olivia rummages through her backpack, pretending to look for . . . something. Anything. "Oh," she says finally, "who cares? You can have him."

Brittany grimaces. "I don't want him."

"Then let's take him to the pound and have him put to sleep."

Olivia used to be funny, but in a kind of jack-in-the-box way: cute but no real surprises. Now she's more sarcastic: a jack-in-the-box with a poison nose.

She likes to make people laugh. Or gasp. Maybe because she depends on others more and wants to reward them. They have to do things for her, like open doors and reach where she can't. If there's an earthquake or a fire or a terrorist attack and she's upstairs, somebody (or two somebodies) has to pick her up and tote her out of the building. She likes the word *tote*. Isn't there an old song or poem where somebody has to lift a barge and tote a bale? She's a kind of bale now. One half of which happens to move.

Kent's probably tired of opening doors, tired of having half a girlfriend. Somebody who's always sitting down.

Olivia can go outdoors, but not like she used to. She's in a chair. Seated. Sure, she's seen those crippled guys who play murderball or who careen downhill in the wheelchair part of the marathon. But wheels or no wheels, if you're in a chair, you're sitting down. A chair is a place to read. A place at a table with some other chairs. A place to rest. Just not forever.

She's thought about what she'll do when a fire is raging and the building is shaking and terrorists are standing outside with machine guns and anthrax while people like Kent run down the stairs. Leaving her alone.

All she can do is fall out of her chair and crawl down the steps like a reptile. When she told her mother this, she said, "You're not going to be crawling anywhere like anything. Not while I'm alive."

Olivia can imagine her mom leaping over the earthquake's brand-new chasms and knocking over terrorists to get to her. Maybe knocking over Kent, too.

Olivia was literally crushed by her accident, but her father was emotionally crushed. (He's recovering in Santa Fe with a new wife. And a new daughter. Who walks.) Somehow the accident made her mother stronger. She went to rehab with Olivia. She learned everything about paraplegia. She got a job. She dated. A little, anyway. For companionship more than anything else. Somebody to have coffee with. Somebody to talk to on the phone.

But if things started to get serious and Mr. Man of the Moment took one look at Olivia and thought, *Way too much baggage, man,* her mom read his mind and he was out of there. Good-bye, Harrison Ford. Her mom called them all Harrison Ford because in the movies he was always coming to somebody's rescue, saving her life, then making out like crazy.

Olivia thought of the making out she'd done. Just kissing at parties. How, because of the wheelchair, the boy had to lean over her like a waiter in a noisy restaurant. Or he had to fetch something so he could sit beside her.

Olivia had the Chair Test. The dumb ones sat beside her like they were on a bus. The smart one — there had only been one — turned his chair the other way so they were kind of face-to-face. It was almost like standing up.

When it came to those parties, she felt like an intruder, anyway. Or at least like she didn't belong. Her friends seemed to like her, and the boys didn't seem to mind kissing sitting down. But she couldn't help feeling different. If her friends were lamps, she was a lantern. Almost the same, but not quite.

A passing bell rings and Olivia tells Brittany they'll hook up at lunch. It's not Brittany's fault she can walk, but why did Kent have to call *her*? Olivia wasn't going to cry. It's just too stupid. She might as well get used to being dumped.

She pushes herself toward the bathroom, which is at the west end of the long hall decorated with long banners. GOOD-BYE, MS. MARVEL is the latest. Olivia's friends painted those for a teacher who's leaving. They rolled butcher paper out on the edge of the soccer field, then wrote with big brushes.

That was something else Olivia couldn't do well. Try writing GOOD-BYE from a wheelchair! "Do the first letter," one of her girlfriends said, "and I'll do the rest." But watching everybody leaning and kneeling and springing to their feet and dipping their brushes just made Olivia want to write something really rude.

When she gets to the bathroom, she just stares at the door. It opens the right way, not toward her, but it's still hard. It for sure isn't one of those cool electric ones with a button the size of a dinner plate. It's just an old-fashioned, kind of narrow, kind of heavy door. For most people a way in, but for Olivia it's just in the way.

So she sits there until someone comes along. There's this game she plays while she waits: Puppy from Hell. Because animals have to wait for someone to open the door. Then someone does and pats them on the head. People do that to her sometimes. They pat her on the head. And when they do, she goes for the throat. Verbally, anyway. People in wheelchairs hate to be patted! People in wheelchairs aren't pets.

While she waits, she also eyes the trophy cases that line this part of the hall. She can see the silver and gold. The tiny runners on top. The basketball and football and soccer players.

Then she spots the trophies for people like her. Special

people. Differently abled. Challenged. Olivia hates *challenged*. It used to be a cool word for things like duels. Now if somebody's nose runs, he's nasally challenged and gets a government grant. For God's sake—she's a person in a wheelchair. What's so special about that?

"Hey, Olivia."

She looks up. "Hey, Gloria."

Gloria holds the bathroom door, then goes to the mirror and frowns at herself. She's got the biggest boobs in seventh grade. It's all the boys talk about. Probably all Kent talks about. Gloria can have him. They're perfect for each other. Him with his precious trumpet and her with her crop-top and her low-slung jeans—half-naked from you-know-where down to you-know-where.

Olivia refuses to care which pair of khakis she takes out of her closet. Her mother wants to shop at J.Crew, but Olivia is happy with the Gap. The point isn't brand names. Not to show her useless legs—that's the point.

Sometimes she wishes she didn't look the same every day. It isn't exactly a uniform, but in a way it is. Like the Goths. Except that she's a Cripple. The clique nobody wants to belong to.

What she doesn't wear is jeans. She had on jeans the day of the accident. Once they got her to the hospital, they cut them off her.

It isn't just that jeans remind her of the accident, either. Jeans are outdoor pants. Doing things pants.

Bending, walking, squatting, kicking things pants. And she doesn't do that anymore. Never.

Gloria is still working on her lip gloss when Olivia takes the quarter out of her purse, the quarter she made sure she had when she left home. She reaches for the slot in the tampon machine. In another mirror she sees Gloria glance, then unglance. Gloria wants nothing to do with this.

Well, Olivia doesn't want a lot to do with it either. This thing with her period is so unfair. Nothing works down there, not really. Not like it should. But every month there's a period. Why? Nobody's going to marry her. She's not going to have kids. If something had to work, why couldn't it be her bladder?

But oh, no. She can't even feel when she has to go. It just trickles out any old time. Right onto the chair, right onto the floor. Or it could if she let it. If she didn't have a catheter and a tube and a bag.

Isn't that romantic? Sometimes her mother has a couple of glasses of chardonnay and they do this routine where Olivia is Olivia and her mother is a boy. Olivia says, "Just a minute, darling. Let me slip out of this old wheelchair and into an empty urine bag." And her mother replies in a deepish voice, "It doesn't matter, sweetheart. I love you just the way you are."

What a crock. Nobody could love her just the way she is.

Olivia finishes in the bathroom and is washing her hands when a girl she's seen around but doesn't really know walks in, says hi, then pulls a couple of paper towels out of the dispenser and hands them to her.

What is this — Help the Handicapped Week?

The girl fools around with her hair in the mirror, smiles at Olivia again, and turns toward the door. "See you, kid," she says. And she pats Olivia on the head.

"Woof," Olivia says. She lets her tongue hang out. "Woof, woof, woof."

All she gets is a scrunched-up, bewildered face and a speedier exit. Olivia can't help but notice how thin the girl is and how cute her jeans are. She can imagine the girl buying those jeans, looking at herself in the mirror, glancing over her shoulder to see if they were tight enough. Imagine never seeing your butt in a mirror again.

That's why Olivia is glad she went off on that girl. Got over on her. Let her know that she knew. Called her on it. Olivia knows from watching Animal Planet that everybody is either predator or prey. She knows she looks like prey now — slow and semihelpless. But she isn't. She's a lone wolf. Now, anyway, for sure.

There's English before lunch, so she goes there. Or in that direction, anyway, taking the long way. The one that doesn't go by Kent's locker.

A wheelchair is the all-time hall pass. She can always take her time. Like today she slows down and glances into the copy room. There are usually two or three teachers standing there with a quiz or an exam they need thirty clones of. Today, though, there's only one man — hair in a ponytail, corduroy pants, a denim shirt, and Birkenstock sandals with woolly socks. She pictures him eating granola and drinking something green.

When she gets to class, someone has written on the board *Mr. Sterling Is Ill. Wait for Sub.*

Immediately she imagines herself waiting for a submarine. Palm trees, white sand, her in a one-piece bathing suit, long tanned legs. It's just a brief dream, but like the more complicated ones at night, she's walking. Just that. Not going anywhere special. Not kicking field goals or scoring in soccer. Merely walking. .

While Brittany settles in at the desk beside her, Olivia wonders if Mr. Sterling is really ill. Or does he just need a mental health day like everybody else? She tries picturing him with a cold or an upset stomach. She tries to imagine him lying down, but he stands up and starts talking about two roads diverging in a yellow wood. He can get up like that even when he's sick, because whatever he has is just temporary.

Just then the door opens and the man from the copy room comes in. He looks flustered. Without saying anything, he erases the board and writes his name, stopping once to change an *e* to an *i*. Mr. Kline. Not Mr. Klene.

With his back to them, the kids look at one another. The seat of Mr. Kline's pants is shiny; he has that stupid ponytail, and those sandals. Kent half stands up, turns, and puts one finger to his lips. The Silent Treatment. They can't say even one word to this substitute teacher.

As Mr. Kline calls the roll, everyone raises his or her hand. When he gets to Olivia, he asks, "Would you like to sit closer to the board?"

She replies, "I'm crippled, Mr. Clean. Not blind."

Everybody loves that. While Mr. Kline blushes and stammers, Kent turns and grins at her. Olivia gives him her best glare. Who cares that he was the only one who passed the Chair Test at that party and was a good kisser, too. Whatever made her think he could really like her?

At noon, Olivia makes her way to the cafeteria. She's mad at everything and everybody. There are way too many of those dopey Hello Kitty backpacks, and the ones that look like roadkill-with-straps aren't a whole lot better. Some days it's like everybody's got the same T-shirt with THE CLASH scrawled across it. Or baggy button-downs from somebody's dad or the thrift store. And just forget about the mean-looking belts and leather wristbands from the Bad Boy Boutique.

Her lunch, wrapped in a wrinkled paper sack, is deep in her backpack. A lot of kids bring their lunches, but Olivia pretty much has to. It's such a hassle to get in line. She can't reach up and over to get the tacos or the mac-and-cheese or the baked apple. She can barely point because she can't see over the steam tables, which are at eye level. Everybody else's eye level. It's all just food to her. Something steaming in a big aluminum tray. And the one time Kent helped her was kind of humiliating. He had to rattle off the choices and she had to remember and then choose. He wasn't a boyfriend; he was a waiter. He was supposed to say, "You look nice today. I like that sweater." Not "The special today is fish sticks."

So she goes right to the table where she always sits, and Brittany brings her a carton of milk. That's fine, that's something anybody might do for anybody.

She says hi to everybody and looks at their trays. What's that black-and-white thing—penguin? She's glad to take out her wrinkled bag. The one her mother can't stand. The one Olivia insists on using because it's pathetic. There she is—with a ratty old lunch bag decorated with grease spots. And no boyfriend.

While she eats lunch, she listens to the other girls. They say they want to be CEOs or doctors or astronauts, but when there aren't any parents or teachers around, all they talk about is boys. What boys say and who they say it to. What some boy is wearing and how it makes him look. The way somebody stands or sits, the color of his eyes or hair or socks.

Then they agree that boys are stupid. If they didn't carry those lame skateboards everywhere. If they didn't talk about PlayStation so much. If they weren't always punching each other.

Only Gloria—the one with the boobs who just

happens to be sitting at the table today because Gloria is kind of a lunch hour nomad—doesn't join in the general trashing of boys.

"I was with my dad the other day," Gloria says in a whisper that carries the length of the table, "and when we went by Randy Bishop's house, he was washing his dad's Toyota and he was so cute."

Randy is cute. Olivia might as well like him now because all she can do for the rest of her life is like boys who would never like her back.

"Look who's coming," warns Brittany.

Oh, God. It's Mary Elizabeth Norton. Little Miss Goody Two Wheels.

"I heard what you said in English." Mary Elizabeth bumps her wheelchair into Olivia's. "And that was so mean. It's hard being a substitute teacher."

"I'm sorry," said Olivia. "I'll try and be better. More like you."

Mary Elizabeth acts all exasperated, then rolls away, shaking her head. She's pretty in a kind of dopey-doll way. Her accident was only three years ago; Olivia's was six. But Mary Elizabeth has adjusted. If anything, she does more than before. More clubs, more activities, more volunteer work.

Olivia says, "She's going to braid ribbons that match the ones in her hair through the spokes in her wheelchair. And then she's going to all the dances and her date is going to turn her in circles and everyone's going to say how brave she is."

Brittany frowns. "If Kent asks, would you go?"

Olivia shakes her head. "No way. Forget about him."

"If somebody you liked better asked?"

"I'm not going to dances, period."

Brittany puts down her tuna sandwich. "Then me neither."

Olivia frowns at her. "Why not? You're not in a wheelchair."

"God, Olivia. Everything's not about your stupid wheelchair."

They both stare down at their plates. Nobody at the table says anything. It wasn't that loud, but it's like everybody in the cafeteria heard.

Then Brittany all of a sudden grips Olivia's wrist. "Oh, my God. Kent looked over here."

Olivia mutters, "He's looking at you, not me. You're the one he called."

"Shut up. He wants to talk to you."

"Well, I don't want to talk to him."

Brittany leans in so close Olivia can smell the tuna on her breath. "Just go toward the door. And give me that stupid paper bag."

"Fine. I was going anyway."

She wasn't, but once she says it then she is, so that makes it true. As she backs away from Brittany and turns around, she knows that all her friends are watching. They want her to get back together with Kent. Or yell at him. They watch a lot of TV, so they want something dramatic to happen. Anything.

Just past the jocks' table, she catches a glimpse of Kent closing in on her. OK—she'll let him hold the door for her. And she does. Then he follows her up the hall, walking right beside her.

"That was cool in English today," Kent says.

Olivia brushes that away and goes right to the heart of the matter. "Listen, I already talked to Brittany."

"About what?"

She looks up at him. He's so gangly. His feet are so big. His nose is so long. His backpack is so huge. He's so cute. "About how you broke up with me."

"*I* broke up with *you*? A couple of days ago I e-mailed you three pages; you wrote back two lines."

"That's the night I had an earache. And, anyway, I think it's silly to play the trumpet over the phone. How can you hold the phone and play, too?"

"I don't hold the phone; I lay it down. Or put it on speaker."

"So did you play the trumpet for Brittany?"

"No. I only play with Jeremy. We might start a garage band and his mom won't let him stay out late, so we practice on the phone."

"In the garage?"

"Not yet exactly. We're in our bedrooms."

"So you've got a bedroom band."

People pass them, people who look or don't look. When Olivia's girlfriends come out of the cafeteria, they act like she and Kent are invisible.

He steps closer to her. Before he can lean on her wheelchair in that way she just loves, she says, "You're the one who told Brittany you weren't my boyfriend anymore."

"Well, you're the one who's been acting weird. You're the one who hung up real fast. I figured you were tired of me. I was hoping Brittany would tell me why."

"Listen, Kent. Nobody wants a girlfriend in a wheelchair."

He stops and tugs at the straps of his backpack like he's carrying a heavy load. "Man, Olivia. What is with you and that wheelchair? I never think about it. And why should I? You think about it enough for both of us."

She looks at her lap. Her more or less numb, useless lap.

Kent says, "Fine! I'm gonna shoot hoops after school, Dave and me against these other guys. I need some moral support, but I don't suppose some poor little girl in a wheelchair could make it all the way out to the court."

Then he's gone.

For the rest of the day, Olivia thinks about what Kent said. She thinks about it during math and social studies. She can't concentrate, or maybe she can only concentrate on it. How she's not just using a wheelchair to get places, how *it's* pushing *her* around. Bullying her. Who's in charge here, anyway?

At two thirty she needs to stop at the bathroom and empty her bag again, so she's a little late to the outside court, which is located between the main building and the soccer field. Brit has saved a place for her, so she glides in and puts the brakes on her chair.

Kent and David have changed for the game. They're both in blue shorts and white T-shirts like a team. Their legs are long and white. The guys they're playing against are eighth graders; they're just in their jeans and sneaks. But they're faster and smoother. Olivia can tell that just by watching them warm up.

So in a way, Kent and Dave are handicapped. But all that really means is they're going to have to try harder.

The guys are outgunned from the start. They shoot wildly. The eighth graders blow through their feeble defense. Pretty soon it's 16–4. Then Kent settles down and starts to shoot from outside. He drains two three-pointers in a row.

The seventh-grade girls chant, "David, David, he's our man. If he can't do it, Kent can."

Olivia joins in, clapping and yelling. As Kent sets up for a shot, one of the older guys charges, so he passes to David, who waits a second too long and has the ball slapped right out of the air.

It bounces hard and heads for the sidelines, right toward the girls. Everybody else screams and ducks. Olivia simply catches the ball.

Kent trots over. He grins down at her. "Good hands, Olivia."

The game starts again. Kent and Dave are down by ten, then seven.

Brittany leans in. "Guess who likes you after all?"

ABOUT THE AUTHOR AND THE STORY

Ron Koertge is a teacher of writing as well as a poet, novelist, and short story writer whose novel *The Arizona Kid* was selected by the American Library Association as one of the 100 Best of the Best Books for Young Adults published between 1967 and 1992. His more recent novels for teens include *Stoner & Spaz,* winner of the PEN West Award for Children's Literature, a German Youth Literature Award Nominee, and a Michigan Thumbs Up! Honor Book, and *Margaux with an X,* an American Library Association Best Book for Young Adults as well as a New York Public Library Book for the Teen Age. He is also the author of two highly praised novels in verse: *The Brimstone Journals,* an ALA Best Book for

Ron Koertge

Young Adults and winner of the Kentucky Bluegrass Award, and *Shakespeare Bats Cleanup,* which appears among *VOYA*'s 2003 Top Shelf Fiction for Middle School Readers.

Koertge's short stories have appeared in several anthologies edited by Don Gallo, including *On the Fringe, Destination Unexpected,* and *What Are You Afraid Of? Stories About Phobias.* In fact, in the phobia anthology's story "Calle de Muerte," you can meet a slightly older incarnation of Olivia as she helps the main character deal with his fear of crossing the street.

As a teacher at Pasadena City College in southern California, Koertge is used to seeing students in wheelchairs. His wife, Bianca, also happens to work with disabled students at the same institution, and so she was an excellent research source for Ron as he wrote about Olivia. "If I wasn't sure about something, I'd just ask her," he says. But, Koertge cautions, this is not a story about how everyone in a wheelchair feels or acts. "The disabled community has every personality type—good-natured, benign, fierce, sarcastic, other-centered, et cetera. Olivia's thorniness or attitude isn't going to be everyone's."

Ron Koertge's latest book of poems is titled *Fever.* The author says this book "isn't for kids necessarily, but it's such an easy read that a teenager should like it." His newest novel, *Deadville,* features Ryan, a slacker who's sleepwalking through life. When the most popular girl at school falls into a coma, Ryan finds himself visiting her every day. It may be that talking to her can wake them both up.

*If love is blind, maybe friendship
can be blind also.*

See You

KATHLEEN JEFFRIE JOHNSON

Huffing and puffing up Wilson Avenue, Jason hurries home from the fish market as he does every Saturday morning with a paper-wrapped package of raw fish tucked under his plump arm.

Should he stop at Starbucks? It's just a few blocks ahead. It always smells great — *soooo* much better than the dank, stinky fish market — and he'd really like something sweet and delicious with coffee and chocolate and whipped cream swirling around in his mouth *right now*. Doesn't he deserve a reward for climbing Wilson? But he's got to keep moving because of the stupid fish, and besides, he doesn't even know how to order, doesn't know which coffee is called which, or what size is big—

Venti? Grande? What idiot came up with those names? Everybody will laugh at him standing there with his mouth open trying to read the menu quickly, trying to order what he wants and not a cup of *green tea* like he ended up with last time, scurrying out the door before anyone could see his red face and say the names—

Forget it. It's crap; everything is crap.

He continues his hustle through downtown Fairmont—the small, worn-down, grimy city where his parents left him six years ago with his grandmother—plagued with his usual evil thoughts. *They dumped me! It's called ABANDONMENT, people!*

He glares at a woman jogging past in running shorts, her face red and her hair frizzled. Does she care that he was left behind? Of course not. Lots of people are in town this morning, hogging up the sidewalks for the stupid spring festival—but does any one of them care? No. They think he's doing just fine.

Jason watches as a really tall, skinny, gray-haired man tries to fold himself and a six-pack into a tiny compact car parked in front of Bud's Beer. Care? Nope.

Jason's willing to concede one point to the so-called authorities: his parents are druggies and thieves. They vacation in the slammer! But living with his grandmother isn't much better. She gives him the *death stare* if he so much as burps at the table. She says if he's not careful, he'll end up in either jail or hell, whichever comes first, just like his mother and father.

His mother! His father! Jason can barely contain his disgust.

Why couldn't they have dumped him in Los Angeles or Las Vegas, where he could have been adopted by somebody rich and cool? Where people wear sunglasses all day and all night and no one can even *see* you if you don't want to be seen, where—

Shitzu! It's *Hadley.*

Hadley, with her perfect body and her long, blond hair, rushes down the sidewalk toward him, arm in arm with her best friend, Lisa, the two of them laughing out loud. Hadley's face is so red it's like she's got a sunburn, except she's a *cheerleader.* Cheerleaders don't get sunburned; they get tan. She's just laughing hard at something mean. She's in his American history class, and if she sees him, she'll laugh at *him.*

Pleasepleaseplease don't let her see me, pleasepleaseplease.

The names crowd into his head. *Lard Butt. Piggie. Fish Face.*

In an unexpected moment of inspiration, Jason turns smartly into the doorway of the Cigar Shoppe and tensely studies the HOURS OF BUSINESS, the indentation of the entrance just enough to remove him to the far edge of Hadley's perfect universe, just out of sight, so *pleasepleaseplease* out of mind—and it works! They continue past.

They turn left on Woodmont, giggling. They don't see him; he's safe.

Thank you thank you thank you, he sings to the Great Whatever. But really, now that he has His (Hers? Its?) attention, *Why couldn't You have put me someplace else, not in a craptown like Fairmont, filled with beady-eyed grandmothers and all-purpose meanies?*

Why?

"Anybody here speak *blind?*"

Tyler grips his cane and listens—to exactly nothing. OK, so nobody's answering. His little joke about being blind didn't work. He's alone.

He knew that.

The *whoosh-spin* of moving traffic is absent. There's a horn blaring in the distance, but no cars are passing nearby. So he's not standing on Wilson. Well, of course he isn't. There are always plenty of people on Wilson. Someone would have answered, would have given him the information he needed—like, where is he?

He let Hadley spin him around like a top, take his arm, and pull him—*pull him!*—down the street and across the intersection and even farther, like he was a dog on a leash. A freakin' dog!

Tyler adjusts his sunglasses, which he wears mostly to guard his eyes. That, and the fact that everyone says they look good on him. It's overcast today, though, so there's no sun on his face to help with direction. Not that that usually works anyway. Still . . .

The absence of voices is admittedly strange. There's a lot more people in town this morning than usual, here for the Fairmont Spring Festival, so you'd think someone would be around, even on a side street off Wilson. The festival is supposed to start — he presses the button on his watch, which announces *9:46 a.m.* — at ten o'clock, on Marshall Plaza, with a parade.

He wants to avoid the parade, and the crowded sidewalks it will bring.

Not that he's exactly in a crowd now.

He'd been standing, waiting to cross Wilson at Fifth, when Hadley, smelling of honeysuckle, her laughter as bright as sweetly chiming bells, intercepted him. He'd gladly let her pull him along for a good block, maybe two, weaving in and out of people angling for a spot to view the passing show, before they'd crossed, but now —

As they'd scrambled down the sidewalk he'd smelled the delicious odor of coffee wafting out of Starbucks, so he knew he was on Wilson then. They'd slowed down and taken their time passing *that* shop — he knew exactly where it was — but how long ago, in terms of time and space, was that? He can't smell it now. And again, where's the traffic? And all the people hustling over to the food and craft booths set up at Marshall Plaza? People lining up for the parade. The ones who had kept blocking him on his way home.

The festival doesn't interest him, but even Fairmont High has booths set up, one of them a cake sale sponsored by the cheerleaders. Which has to be why Hadley's around.

He pulls up the collar of his jacket. Where is she, anyway?

She'd clung to his arm like a drowning person clutching a life jacket, and he hadn't corrected her, hadn't said one word of protest.

Of course not! This was *Hadley*. Of the long, blond hair. Tyler can just barely remember long, blond hair. A neighbor, when he was a kid. A girl probably his own age now. Tyler can almost see it, luminous and bright, swaying back and forth as she walked.

That was before the onslaught of volatile juvenile diabetes, and the loss of his vision, when he was seven. A long time ago. Before he became legally blind.

Tyler snorts. OK, totally blind, but so what? Today he's just fine. Really fine. *Hadley* fine!

She sits in front of him in American history, her silky hair draped over the back of her chair, long enough to caress his cassette recorder, his hand—sometimes he even wraps a smooth strand around his finger, just for an instant or two, letting it slip off before she knows what he's done.

The last time, her hair had smelled like coconut.

Like *heaven*.

But she's a cheerleader, so of course she smells like

coconut, like lilacs or roses. She's *gorgeous*—everybody says that. His fingers—his body!—are completely and utterly willing to verify the facts. And didn't she just break up with her dud-stud boyfriend, Kurt? He'd been caught squeezing a new girl or something. Everybody was yabbering about it at school yesterday. *Poor Hadley.* Poor thing and all that.

Except that meant she was free. She wasn't Tyler's usual sort, but he'd had his accomplishments with girls, right? Why not move up?

So when she'd surprised him on Wilson, walking up beside him out of nowhere, saying, "Hi, Tyler," in that lilting tone of hers, asking if she could be of assistance— well, damn right she could! He'd wanted her body as close to his as possible. And she obliged, clinging tightly to his arm. He could even feel the soft edge of her breast. Was she coming on to him? Maybe she was, after the breakup and everything. Maybe she needed a guy who actually knew what to do with the opposite sex. . . .

Which he does, ever since he realized that being blind and good-looking is not an entirely bad combination when it comes to getting girls. Poor Tyler and all that.

He grins. He can't help it.

But he also can't ignore the fact that right now he's both alone and cold. He touches his sunglasses, then folds his cane and tucks it under his arm, shoving his hands into his pockets. He could use some Starbucks right about now. He's careful about managing his diabetes, so today he'd skip the chocolate and whipped cream version of something hot and go for the green tea, which he likes well enough.

He doesn't need Hadley to get around at all, of course. He walks around Fairmont all the time. He knows the streets and the shops; they're laid out in his head like a map. He doesn't need help. He worked out the rules for being blind a long time ago.

Which don't include being pulled around like a poodle, but in truth, he'd been a happy poodle. He would have let her drag him anywhere.

Preferably to someplace private, where he could feel her *entire*—

Then she'd suddenly let go of his arm. "There's the Yarnster. I promised my mom I'd pick up her order. Since I'm here and everything. She's a knitting freak. Be back in"— she giggled, tapping the end of his nose with each word—"Just. One. Minute." She'd pressed herself against his arm for final encouragement, and this time he felt her whole breast. "Don't you move a muscle, OK?"

He hadn't. Grinning to himself, he'd stood still, knowing this was a game, but what a game! This was *Hadley*.

Who, Tyler has to admit—bouncing up and down on his heels to keep warm—still hasn't come back.

He's not standing in front of the Yarnster, that's for sure. There's always a lot of foot traffic and voices in front of it, plus it's right next to Video Blast. Did she think he wouldn't figure that out, like, immediately?

Removing his cane from his armpit, Tyler unfolds it, tapping it lightly back and forth across the pavement, moving forward a couple of steps, touching—absolutely nothing. From the sound the tip of his cane makes, and from the feel of the ground under his shoes, he knows he's on asphalt, not concrete. But he can't be more than a few steps off of Wilson or another street, can he? Is he in an alley? Why would she leave him in an alley?

A parking lot?

He tries to swallow the small rise of fear in his gut.

"Why does Grandma always have to have fresh fish? And why on a *Saturday,* when *I* have to go buy it? Why can't we eat frozen fish sticks from the Food Lion like everybody else?"

Jason says this out loud, just in case the Big Whatever is still listening.

Resuming his trot up Wilson, the slightly stinky package of fresh flounder trapped under his arm, Jason adds, just to himself, *What if I run into somebody else from school? That stupid festival thing is happening. What if I run into somebody and they call me one of those names?*

Well, running into Mary Anne would be OK. She's a cheerleader, too, but she's nice, not quite as pretty as Hadley, maybe, but close enough and *nice*. She doesn't like him either, nobody does, but she doesn't use the names, and one time, when he picked up a pencil she dropped in a crowded hallway at school and handed it back to her, she even smiled at him.

Jason couldn't believe it. She'd smiled at *him*! *Himhimhimhimhim!* For a moment, his universe had intersected with hers, and he'd become *visible*! Jason holds that happy memory for the five seconds it takes to remember where he is. *Alone in Fairmont. Bully bait.*

Looking hurriedly up and down the cross streets, up and down the alleyways, he hustles on. With his luck he'll probably run into Kurt, Hadley's boyfriend, who fries kids like him for breakfast.

Except, didn't they break up? Someone saw Kurt in a lip-lock with Theresa, the captain of the drill team; everybody was talking about it yesterday in school. *Poor Hadley,* the girls all said. *Poor thing.*

Nobody talks to Jason, but that doesn't mean he doesn't have eyes and doesn't have ears. And, he shouts silently to the Great Whatever, *You might try speaking a little louder, too. What am I anyway, chopped liver?*

Or chopped fish. NOT! Jason gives the package a quick squeeze, just to let everybody know who's boss, but there's only a dead flounder present to experience this manly display of strength.

Jason weaves through the upsurge of Saturday-morning people in town for the stupid festival, probably investigating the crappy sales thrown by the crappy shops in honor of the big, crappy event. No kids yet, besides Hadley and Lisa, so that's good, just— *huh*?

Jason stops cold, looking down the driveway that leads to the back lot behind what used to be the tiniest car dealer in the world, Guston's Used Cars, now boarded up. The lot, surrounded by the backs of various businesses, some open, more shut forever as Fairmont continues its long slide into decline, is an enclosed square. Jason stood there with his grandmother two years ago, when she bought her latest previously owned Ford.

So what's the blind kid doing there? Jason can just see him beyond a bunch of piled-up branches, cut bushes, and tree limbs that somebody dumped at the back of the drive, leaving a small passageway. *Tyler.* Tapping the asphalt with his white cane like he's a wizard or something. Jason shudders.

The blind kid doesn't use the names, but he sits two seats over from Jason in American history and has never even once said hi, which is actually fine because what if he needed help or something? Dropped his cassette recorder or braille book, or couldn't find his way to his next class, or tripped over his stupid cane? What would Jason be required to do? Help him? He doesn't know how to help him! He doesn't want to help anyone or do anything.

Besides, Tyler doesn't need any help. He gets around fine; he's good-looking; girls like him. *Why did you have to waste good looks on a blind person,* he asks the Big Whatever, *when I didn't get* anything? Tyler's disabled *and* handsome, plus he gets all the attention. It isn't fair!

So Tyler doesn't need Jason's help, and besides, he's full of himself, with the looks and the girls thing.

Jason waits at the next corner while a car barrels past. How does a blind person cross when there's no signal? Even if there *is* a signal? Jason can't figure that one out.

This past week—on Wednesday—he saw Tyler lightly touching the back of his hand against Hadley's hair, then wrap a strand around his finger. And sniff it! Is he a pervert or something? You don't think of blind people being perverts. Though if it was going to happen, Fairmont would be the place.

Now, Mary Anne's hair—

Shivering, Jason scurries ahead, concentrating on fish sticks, which are so much easier to think about than blind people and creeps and Mary Anne's hair, shiny and dark and . . .

Fish sticks fish sticks fish sticks

Jason likes his with Tater Tots, the whole of it doused with a big galumph of bright red ketchup—God's personal gift to him. So see, he got *something*. He's not a total *nothing*. God doesn't make junk—he's heard that somewhere—and ketchup is proof.

He just wants to get home *with no names* and sit in front of his PlayStation, the big, *really* big, surprise birthday gift from his father on his last swing through town between jail gigs. Where did he get the money? Jason doesn't want to know. But for some reason his father remembered, HELLO, that he had a son. So the

PlayStation first, then the TV for golf. (Why does he like golf? Jason doesn't know. He's never played it, probably never will.) Followed by *Sea Space: Black Hole Pirates*—he's on the third book in the series. And for the entire day he'll be invisible, he'll disappear, pleasantly and comfortably, from Fairmont.

Until the reek of baked flounder invades and totally karate-chops his nose and he's forced to stop eating potato chips and root beer and chocolate-chip cookies and has to sit down with his grandmother at her formally set dining-room table—a tablecloth! real silver! goblets!—and eat baked fresh fish and boiled potatoes and hideous green beans, and if he so much as *thinks* of the ketchup bottle, he gets the death stare.

"I *indulge* you, Jason," his grandmother says firmly, holding him in the grip of her steely, pale-blue eyeballs, "every day of the week. Indulge me just this once. A little culture never hurt anyone."

So, to avoid the death stare, he cuts up his fish using *both* his knife and fork, chews the beans with his mouth shut, dots his lukewarm spuds with little pats of butter that don't melt, and hates Fairmont with all his heart.

By the time Tyler hits the Dumpster with his cane, he knows he's in a back lot of some kind, but where? And why can't he find the entrance, where he came in with Hadley? It doesn't make sense. The lot isn't big, but it's not small. It's medium maybe. He passed some bushes; they must be at the back of a building, possibly in a garden or something. A strip of foliage behind a store. Though why would it be *behind* a store?

How could he be this much off his mark? This doesn't happen to him, ever. No way he's using his cell to call for help. Rule number one for being blind is FIGURE IT OUT! He just needs to get himself oriented.

Sweat moistens his armpits, even though the air is still chilly. He'll just start over. *Persevere*. That's his private code. Nobody dumps *him* into the great unknown and gets him all worked up. *Nobody*. He passed the scared part of being blind years and years ago.

Except his throat tightens as something—*fear*—crawls into his belly, slimy and slippery, squeezing his gut and sending a shuddery panic over his skin, a sweaty, dank claustrophobia gripping him hard. He holds himself rigid, determined to fight it off. No way he's going to stand here like a frightened little kid, like the one he really was in those early days long ago, when he went from full vision to none. When he first went blind.

Afraid to move. Practically crawling across the floor of his bedroom. Hindered by the slightest obstacle. Crashing into furniture and doors. Too terrified to go outside. Clinging to his parents, grabbing on to his older brother, Hollis. Unable to keep up. Isolated. Alone with his fear. *Alone alone alone*. Without a single friend who understood.

With, however, a brother who tripped Tyler when

their parents weren't looking. Who rearranged stuff in Tyler's bedroom, then laughed at the results.

Hollis. Tyler's mouth twists bitterly. Hollis is human now; he's even apologized for being such a butthole when they were kids. Says he was jealous of all the attention Tyler was getting. Jealous! Maybe.

But back then . . . Tyler, feeling the old panic, makes himself inhale, deeply.

If nothing else, Hollis taught him to watch his back.

Things improved enormously when Tyler's parents put him in a special school, where he learned how to take care of himself, how to be blind in a sighted world. Learned how to see with his fingers and feet and ears and nose. With his cane. Learned how to be just another guy.

He became strong enough to thwart, not to mention ignore, Hollis. He made new friends. He left fear behind.

There's no way he's going back now.

Tyler continues taking deep breaths and begins to relax, the tension leaving his muscles. He's OK now. He just needs to figure it out and do it.

He starts around the lot again, the cane his fingers. His eyes.

Jason freezes. Kurt, Hadley's ex-boyfriend, storms down the sidewalk like he just got out of prison and is looking to kill the person who put him there, the scowl on his face as dark as midnight, the snarl on his lips—

Jason's legs turn to lead, fear nailing his feet to the ground.

Stupid! Standing here and staring! What if Kurt sees him? *Oh pleasepleaseplease don't let him see me, pleasepleaseplease—*

Jason whirls to dive into a doorway, but it's not indented and he bangs hard into the thick glass door of the Drug Mart, clobbering his nose and forehead. He yelps, blinking stupidly, then spins around and—

"You!"

Aghhhhh! Kurt has him! By the arm! *Help!* Jason squirms in his grasp, caught like a flounder on a hook, like the real fish smashed under his armpit.

Kurt jerks him close, pulling him by the front of his jacket till they're nose to nose. "You go to Fairmont. Right, Lard Butt?" His breath reeks of coffee.

Jason, barely able to breathe, squeaks out a "Yes." *Let me gooooooooooooooo!*

"You seen that blind kid?"

"Bl-bl-blind kid?" *Porky! I'm stuttering like Porky! What if he calls me Porky?* Sweat rolls down Jason's burning face like tears.

Kurt presses Jason's back against the front window of the Drug Mart. "I need to find that blind kid. He was coming this way. You had to see him. Where is he?"

"Don't know," Jason whimpers. His eyes dart down Wilson and then back to Kurt's face.

Kurt relaxes his grip and grins. "You *do* know. You just looked."

But—

Kurt laughs and grabs Jason's arm, torpedoing him down Wilson, back in the direction Jason's just traveled.

"He was messing with Hadley," Kurt mutters to himself, as if he can't quite believe it. Then, shouting at an elderly man hobbling his way up the sidewalk, "Nobody messes with Hadley!" The man, his thin white hair plastered to his skull, cringes, then ducks into a shop.

Jason, continuing the plunge down Wilson, lets out a silent *eep* of sympathy.

"I'm sitting in the john at Starbucks," Kurt mumbles, as if Jason wasn't even there, "and when I come out—" He stops short, whirling Jason around to face him. "When I come out, my buddy says he's just seen that crappy little blind runt pulling Hadley down the street. He was all over her! Nobody touches Hadley," he yells, spraying Jason's face with spit. "She's mine! Got it?"

Jason nods vigorously, then finds himself once more launched downhill.

He can already feel a bruise starting on his arm. He's in the death grip of a monster! He tries to keep the mashed flounder wedged under his other arm. If he drops it, his grandmother will kill him. Either way he's a goner, he's—

"I thought you and Hadley broke up," he gasps, remembering Theresa, the drill team captain, his tippy toes barely scraping the sidewalk as Kurt hauls him along.

Kurt stops cold and pulls him around, going nose to nose once more, once more blasting Jason with horrible coffee breath. "Listen, Fish Face. Some jerk told Hadley I was messing with another chick. A lie! I find that SOB and he's dead. Got it?"

Jason nods emphatically. *Yes yes yes!*

"Good. Now let's move."

Jason wishes *he* smelled like coffee, even horrible-breath coffee, and not like fear and sweat and flounder. But he reeks of misery. He sees that Guston's Used Cars is coming up, the driveway looming. What should he do? *What should he do?* Tyler's blind! He's full of himself but he's blind. You're not supposed to kill somebody who's blind—

As they pass the alley, Jason sneaks a look. Maybe Tyler is gone by now. Why was he hanging around there anyway? Why—

They stop moving. Kurt has followed his eyes. Kurt is smiling. Kurt shakes Jason off and steps into the driveway.

Jason rubs his arm. He can see Tyler, working his cane. Then Tyler disappears as Kurt moves toward the back lot and fills up all space. *Oh no no no no no no no!*

*   *   *

Footsteps! She's back. Except—

No way those big feet are Hadley's.

Whoever it is, he's coming through the bushes. Shoving them aside. Clutching his cane, Tyler can hear them skitter and scrape across the pavement. The bushes are fake! How could he have missed—

"You!" Kurt barks.

Fear ices Tyler's spine. "Uh, who—"

He gasps as Kurt grabs his jacket and pulls him close, his breath stinking of coffee. "You know damn well *who*. You stay away from Hadley, you hear?" Tyler's throat constricts. "You keep your hands off of her!" Kurt shakes Tyler like a doll.

"Let go!" Tyler cries, trying to shove Kurt away. "My hands weren't on her! She was on me!" He punches wildly, dropping his cane, panic bludgeoning his brain.

"Liar! When I'm through with you, your eyes aren't the only thing that aren't gonna work! You'll wish—"

Tyler shrieks as he's shoved backward, slamming into the ground, the huge, crushing weight of Kurt tumbling down on top of him, pinning him down, banging his sunglasses into his nose. He can't breathe! He's dying!

"Get off of me!" Kurt shouts, his words garbled, trying to shove himself away from Tyler and at the same time lose whatever's clinging to his back. He grabs the plump arm hooked around his neck.

"Quit killing him!" Jason screams, terrified, hanging on, the heat from Kurt's body burning him up. Grandma always says he's going to hell, and she's right; he's there. "Let him alone! You can't kill blind people!"

Kurt rams him in the gut with his elbow, and Jason goes *oof,* collapsing like a popped balloon, sagging to the ground, as out of breath as the dead flounder he dropped somewhere along the driveway in his headlong rush to save Tyler.

They all roll away from one another. Kurt rubs his neck. Tyler curls up sideways on the ground, gasping, hands clutching his legs. Jason has no feeling in his body anywhere. He starts to sit up but freezes when he catches Kurt staring at him. *Oh, no!* He flops back down flat on his back and shuts his eyes, playing dead.

Kurt unexpectedly laughs. "Not bad, Lard Butt!"

Jason blinks, cautiously lifting his head.

"I didn't know you had it in you." Kurt licks blood from a scrape on his palm, then blots it on his jeans. "I was just fooling with him, though. Nothing serious."

Jason sits up, astonished. "Really?"

Kurt sniffs. "Sure. No blind twerp could seriously put the moves on Hadley. She's just fooling with *me,* messing with my head." He laughs. "She must have known I was in Starbucks. Sweet!" He gives Jason a wink. "She's trying to make me jealous because of Theresa. And it worked. God, I love that about her." He grins.

Ooooooookay. Jason knows it's definitely time to leave Fairmont. Steal out of town by night and keep going, head straight for Las Vegas. Just as soon as he can stand up . . .

Tyler gropes determinedly for his cane. Jason reaches for it, but Kurt grabs it first, lumbering to his feet. He waves the long stick around, whipping it through the air like a long, frail sword. Tyler gets up, swaying slightly on his feet.

"So," Kurt says, putting the cane in Tyler's hand, "are we cool, dude?"

"Cool?" Rage explodes in Tyler's gut. Kurt knocks him down and they're *cool*? Treats him the way Hollis used to and they're *cool*? Tyler's hands shake so much he almost drops his cane. Screw Kurt!

Tears sting his eyes. *The rules of being blind, dammit!* They don't include crying like a baby—thank God for his sunglasses. Tyler rubs his hand across his mouth. This isn't a jealous brother. This is *Kurt*. Who has a reputation to maintain. And the fists to back it up. Tyler swallows hard. "Yeah. Sure. We're cool."

"OK, then." Kurt saunters away, disappearing down the driveway.

"That guy's insane." Tyler coughs to hide the break in his voice. "Certifiable." He turns as Jason pulls himself up. "Where am I, anyway?"

"Behind Guston's Used Cars." Jason rubs his arm where Kurt embedded his handprint. "In the back lot."

Tyler laughs sharply. "Guston's! OK, I get it now." How could he have missed that? *Idiot.* He brushes off the seat of his pants. "So you didn't want Kurt to kill me because I'm blind?"

Jason swallows. "Well, yes. I mean, sure."

"But if I hadn't been blind, it would have been OK?"

"Um." This, Jason decides, is when people turn evil. When they ask him *trick questions*.

Tyler shakes his head. "Forget it, Jason." Sighted people can be so incredibly *stupid*. Tyler starts tapping his cane back and forth on the pavement, searching for the exit route. Waiting for Jason to ask what sighted people always ask: How does he know who he's talking to?

"This way." Jason kicks several branches to the side.

"Why are all these fake bushes here?"

"They're not fake. Somebody just trimmed a bunch of branches and trees and stuff, probably sprucing things up for the festival, and dumped it all back here." He shoves the brush, clearing a wide path, in the process discovering — he's got muscles! Something he hadn't really thought about before, sitting in front of his PlayStation. But of course he's got muscles. He jumped Kurt! He's a *hero*. Jason — the Avenger of the Blind! Jason, the —

Wait a minute. "You called me Jason."

Tyler snorts. "Isn't that your name?"

Jason stares at Tyler. "Kurt didn't say it. Neither did I."

Tyler laughs. "I recognized your voice. I've got ears, you know." *Plus you breathe through your mouth like a fish, and Kurt called you Lard Butt.* "You sit two seats over from me in American History." *Sheesh.*

Jason blinks. "You know that?"

"Obviously." Tyler starts moving. "Well, thanks for your help."

Help? "I saved you," Jason blurts.

Tyler stops. "No, you didn't." Why do sighted people always think he needs to be saved?

"Yes, I did. I jumped Kurt and saved you."

"You stepped in, so thanks. But I would have pushed him off. You heard him. He wasn't serious."

"He wasn't serious only because he suddenly had a witness. *Me.* And I jumped him." Jason's chest puffs with pride. He knows bullies. Knows how they operate. He feels like a DA on *Law & Order*.

Tyler is silent. No way he's in debt to a loser like Lard Butt. No way. He's already thanked him. What more does he want? "Yeah, whatever," he mutters, tapping his way down the driveway.

Jason, almost giddy with the happy joy of it all, trots alongside, stopping only to pick up his flounder. He brushes off the smudged paper. Did Kurt step on it? It doesn't look too bad. If Grandma gives him the death stare tonight—he'll give it right back!

They stop when they reach the sidewalk. "So, are we, like, friends now?" Jason almost levitates with excitement. He hasn't had a friend since he was dumped in Fairmont six years ago, since before that, actually. Since—well, forever.

Tyler pauses to orient himself. He needs to turn left, head back up Wilson.

"Are we?" *Are we are we are we?* What will they do first? Go to a movie? Do blind people go to movies?

Tyler adjusts his sunglasses. *Crap.* Does Jason seriously think he wants to be friends with him now? "Um, I don't know."

Oh. Jason had forgotten that nobody likes him, ever. Still . . . he *saved* Tyler! He's Jason the Avenger! "Well, can we at least say hi and stuff?"

Tyler sniffs, then slowly nods. "Sure." He can do that.

Pleased, Jason walks with him up Wilson, the two of them cutting a stream through the now crowded sidewalk, people heading toward Fifth to see the parade.

He warns of a pile of dog poo, so Tyler doesn't step in it.

Tyler thanks him. *Dog shit! The bane of my existence.*

Jason mentions golf, which Tyler says he doesn't play.

Duh, how could I be so stupid? Jason turns the color of a tomato, grateful that Tyler can't see him blush.

"You like ketchup?" Jason asks when they cross Fourth. Ketchup is his last hope.

Tyler laughs. "On everything!" Except he has to be careful about what he eats, since he's a diabetic.

Jason nods in sympathy, then says, "Uh-huh," out loud, remembering that Tyler can't see him. They agree that Tom's Tomato Ketchup Supreme is the best.

When they get to Fifth, Tyler turns left while Jason stands still, the mashed flounder crammed under his arm.

"Bye!" he shouts, waving frantically as Tyler moves into the crowd gathered for the parade. "See you!" he cries as the Fairmont Marching Band begins to screech and wail its way up Fifth.

Tyler pauses a moment, frustrated that he has to maneuver his way through a crowd after all. He *hates* that. Something slimy slithers through his gut once more—

Fear.

Get over it! he shouts silently. *The rules of being blind, dammit!* FIGURE IT OUT! He takes a deep breath. He's probably just in shock from practically getting beaten up. Anyone would feel upset. And isn't he just like anyone?

Yes. It's what he's worked for his whole life.

He's fine now. He just needs to move, part the crowd like Moses parting the sea.

Kurt took him by surprise, that's all. And as for *Hadley*—well, he knows the word that applies. No way he's letting a girl like that get to him again.

Tyler works his cane, people stepping aside so he can get through. Poor Lard Butt. He probably doesn't have any friends at all, probably never will. He's the kind of guy who will always be alone. Scared of his own shadow, and alone.

Alone.

Tyler abruptly swings around, facing the corner where he left Jason. "See you!" he cries, his words lost in the roar of people shouting and applauding as the band heads up Fifth, coming his way.

Kathleen Jeffrie Johnson

ABOUT THE AUTHOR AND THE STORY

Kathleen Jeffrie Johnson, a lifelong resident of the Maryland sub-
urbs of Washington, D.C., is a writer whose next novel is never
anything like her previous ones. Her first book for teens, *The Par-
allel Universe of Liars,* is a provocative story about sex, infidelity,
and lies that was named an American Library Association Quick
Pick. She followed that with *Target,* the extremely painful story
of how a vulnerable sixteen-year-old boy copes after he has been
raped by two strangers. That book was an ALA Best Book for
Young Adults as well as a *VOYA* Top Shelf selection. Next came
A Fast and Brutal Wing, another ALA Best Book for Young Adults
as well as a Knight-Ridder Best Book of the Year and a *VOYA*
2004 Best Science Fiction, Fantasy, and Horror selection. It's a
complex story about personal loss, told as pieces of a puzzle from
multiple perspectives, about a brother and sister who reportedly
can change from human form into animals. More recently, *Dumb
Love,* a lighthearted romance, was selected as a New York Public
Library Book for the Teen Age. Johnson's newest novel, *Gone,* is
about what happens when the only love that seems to be available
is an inappropriate one. When Connor, just turning eighteen, day-
dreams about his former teacher, is she dreaming about him, too?

When asked why she chose to make a blind boy one of her
main characters in "See You," Johnson replied, "Because I'm both
deeply curious about what it is like to be blind and deeply fearful
of being blind, of not having the full use of all my senses. Tyler was
a way to explore, just a little bit, both aspects of my feelings. And

I wrote about Jason because, while not blind, he is someone who is not seen by others. Watching him become more visible was very rewarding."

Johnson notes that blindness can sometimes be a complication of diabetes. Tyler was blinded as a child by an out-of-control case of juvenile diabetes (now often called Type 1 diabetes). She also wants readers to know that careful monitoring of diabetes can help prevent blindness and other complications.

Miguel and Tony are clearly physical opposites,
but they have more in common than they realize.

Fatboy and Skinnybones

RENÉ SALDAÑA JR.

I don't kid myself. I'm a fat guy. Morbidly obese, the doctors call it.

Always have been. Always will be.

Everybody I know calls me *Gordo,* Spanish for Fatboy. Unless, of course, you're my grandma on my dad's side, 'Buela Concha. She calls me *Mi Gordito Lindo,* My Sweet Little Fatboy. To this day (I'm talking about me at close to eighteen and soon to be graduating from high school), the woman still pinches my cheeks when we go visit her on weekends. Hard enough that she leaves red marks.

Even the new kid in school this year on his first day in English class called me fat. He sat in the row of desks next to my table, looked me up and down, side to side, then got every-stupid-body else to giggle if not outright laugh when he said, "Man, you eat the principal, or what, Gordilongo?" Gordilongo's a derivative, I guess. Everybody else thought it was hilarious, including the teacher, who covered a smirk with a fist, and so now they all call me Gordilongo, too.

The kid's one to talk, though. He's got braces with crud stuck all in them and glow-in-the-dark yellow-white pimples ready to burst any minute and pockmarks on the back of his neck; a skinny punk with an Adam's apple the size of a golf ball. But nobody laughs at him; he's too smart for them. Beats them to the punch. Gets them to poke fun at the fat boy instead of at him. Roy, who thinks he's some kind of hotshot, took to him immediately. Sad how a guy'll do almost anything to be in with the cool kids.

Whatever. I'll get over it. I have to, like I always do.

It's nothing new. The way my mother tells it, I've been getting it from the get-go. I was born a big baby. I'm talking huge. So much so, I spent a couple days in the NICU with all the preemies. Doctors wanted to make sure there wouldn't be any serious complications. 'Amá visited me every chance she got. She remembers all the beeping machines keeping track of the other babies' vitals and pipes going in and out of them every which way. Some of them in incubators. But not me. I lay in what's called a radiant warmer, a special crib used to keep babies warm.

According to 'Amá, the nurses took turns changing my diaper. It took two of them to do it. When they were done and thought they were out of earshot, they'd giggle to one another, whispering, "We're calling him Tiny." Meaning it in an ironic and funny way, I guess. "Tiny—it fits." They'd giggle some more. 'Amá was so happy being a new mom she let it slide, *every* time. She should've knocked their blocks off, if you ask me.

My birth certificate states that I was born at fourteen pounds and seven ounces.

When 'Amá tells people this, their eyes grow in amazement. When the initial shock wears off, their lips curl into a sly smile, and they say, without fail, "*Oye* me—that's like one of them frozen turkeys you find at the supermarket coming out of you." They sigh, they look at me like I'm some freak, they say, "You better never be a bad boy to your mother; she carried you—you listening?—she carried you, *this*"—pointing at my gut, some of them (the gall of them) actually reaching out and taking a handful of me—"for nine months." They chuckle, then say to 'Amá, "You deserve some kind of combat medal."

In whispers, they add, "He couldn't have come even a month early to help you out a bit? You're some kind of saint, I tell you. You should put him on a diet. Get him to do some exercise. Play football at school. He'd make a great left tackle." Big as I am, can they not see I'm right there in front of them!

And can't they see I've already lost twenty-five pounds

in the last year? But how could they? They don't know me. They just see what they want to see: a gross, overweight glutton who does nothing but sit around and eat and eat and eat.

'Amá smiles weakly at them. Then she tells me after they've left, "They don't mean any harm, baby. They just don't know any better. But better to smile than to make trouble."

She's a good mother, my mom, but she doesn't get it either. I've been smiling away the pain my whole life long, always taking what others dish out. Behind my back or to my face they'll talk, and I've kept my mouth shut. But I'm sick and tired of turning the other cheek, and everybody and their mom still poking fun. I'll keep up my diet, eat less if I have to; keep working out on 'Amá's exercise bike at home, but go harder now; and wear one of those rubber suits to make me sweat gallons. If I can find one my size. I'll lose so much weight, no one, my mom included, will recognize me. Then even that Skinnybones punk at school will eat his words. And I'm willing to do just about anything to get it done. All I want is to be a regular joe.

So, yesterday I was walking to the supermarket down the street a couple of blocks. This is part of my regimen. I do this at least three afternoons a week, seeing how I work there part-time. I'll tell you what, though: I'm so big I've had to borrow one of the store's shopping carts to lean myself onto and make my way there easier. Otherwise my back would just crumble to bits. But it's a workout.

I can feel the strain on my heart and lungs, and the south Texas heat doesn't help any. 'Amá, as a matter of fact, read that stress like this may even be worse for me because of the exertion. But what else am I going to do? I need some kind of workout, and this is it, really. The bike at home's a joke. I'm too big for it. Besides, I like the time I get to myself walking to work.

I was maybe a half block away when a car pulled up beside me.

"That's quite a load you're carrying there, Gordilongo."

I looked over. It was none other than Pimple-Faced Skinnybones. "Nice ride," I told him, but meant it sarcastically. He didn't get it. He was driving one of those small foreign jobs made up with a ground-effects kit, a spoiler on the trunk, and the funniest paint job I'd ever seen. Almost like he'd done it himself: purple flames along the green side panel that then petered out in sparks or stars or spiky dots. But the paint was textured. I could see the thickness of the brushstrokes.

"You like it?" he said, hanging his left arm out the door and caressing the bad paint.

"Sure," I said. "It's really you." Meaning more loud and showy than cool.

"Thanks. I like it OK. Where you going?" He lowered the volume on some rap music.

"What do you care?" I said. I kept pushing the cart, looking forward mostly.

"Whoa, man. I'm just asking. I'm headed to H.E.B. to start work today. I'm training on the registers. How hard can that be? Take product, scan it, take people's money. A monkey can do that. I heard you work there, too?"

"Yeah, what of it?" Him working the registers meant I'd probably be training him. What kind of cosmic joke was God playing on me?

"That's some chip you got on your shoulder, man. You got to get over whatever it is bothering you."

"You think so?"

"Sure. Like a duck—water off your back. In your case, lots of back, lots of water. He he he." He adjusted the left sideview mirror.

"Drive on, jerk. You don't want to be late on your first day."

"I'd offer you a ride, but, well, I'm already low enough to the ground. And it looks like you're riding low and slow, too." He revved his engine and screeched the back tires, leaving me behind.

What a jerk!

When I got to work, I left my buggy outside and went into the workroom to drop off my lunch. I saw Skinnybones sitting quiet in the corner. He looked up briefly and I noticed his eyes were red, like he'd been crying. He had a produce apron draped over his lap, which was funny because I'd looked at the schedule posted on the door and he was supposed to be training on the register (lucky for me, Mary had been assigned to work with him). I opened my locker and took out my back brace and my specially made stool.

He looked up, then down again.

"What? No joke about the size of the brace, how it can lift a horse, or a house? Nothing about why it is I get to sit down on the job? Fat *and* lazy?" I said.

He shook his head and sniffled.

"What's your problem? Work a bit too much for you already?"

"Shut up, why don't you?" he said.

"Sure I will. Later." *The dude can dish it out, but he can't take it,* I thought.

I left the workroom. I saw Jimmy, the day manager, just outside. He was talking to a couple of guys from produce and one from the bakery. They were all laughing but stopped when they saw me coming. When I got closer, Jimmy said, "Gordo, how's it going?"

I shrugged. "Not much to tell. What's up with the new kid in there?"

"That's what these guys were just telling me about," Jimmy said. "Get this—the kid comes in like he owns the place, telling everybody everything about everything and how he knows it all. Like working a register's beneath him. Luis here told him, 'You've got no clue, kid.' Can you believe it? The kid got in Luis's face and said, 'You got no clue,' and didn't get out of Luis's face."

"Yeah," said Luis. "Real dumb. I mean, look at me."

He was right—all muscle. "I stared at him real mean and said, 'Talk like that? You wanna go outside and back it up?' And I gave him a shove. Just a little one, you know. You should've seen the look in the kid's eyes. It was hilarious. I told him I was only joking, but to watch out who he talked like that to. The next guy might not be so nice."

"So why's he crying?" I asked.

"I scared him so much, I guess, I spooked the pee out of him, literally. He looked down at his legs, then I did, too. He started crying right then. It'd be funnier if it wasn't so sad."

I asked Jimmy if I could see what I could see about the kid. He gave me the go-ahead. So I stepped back into the workroom, set up my stool, and sat opposite the lockers. To my surprise, Skinnybones had pulled off his pants and was over by the sink, running them under the water.

"You know," I said, "girls come in here, too."

"So?" he said. "They don't need to look if they don't want. If they do, then they'll get an eyeful of all of me."

The kid had the skinniest, longest legs I'd seen ever. He had knobs for knees, no sign of muscle anywhere.

"What you looking at?" he said.

"Just looking."

"It's like you've never seen a slender build like mine."

"Slender? That's what you call it?"

"Call it whatever you want to." He was running the wet pants under the heat of the hand dryer now. After a few moments, he started putting them on. "It's all words, man." He wrapped the apron around his waist. "I mean, look at this," he said, pointing at the apron. "It's supposed to be one-size-fits-all. Does this look like it fits? And would it fit you? I don't think so."

The kid was right. The store had to special order mine off the Internet. "So, you going out like that?" I asked.

"Like what?"

"They told me outside you'd peed yourself," I said.

"They got it wrong. They must've meant I was all wet. Or wet behind the ears. It's all words, I tell you." He finished tying the apron on. He looked up at me. "You and me, we're not so different. You know how it goes for people like us. We've got to make do with what we've got." He started out of the workroom, then turned back. "What's your name, anyway?" he asked.

"My name?"

"Yeah, what your mom called you when you were born?"

"It's Miguel. You?"

"Me? I'm Tony, but my friends call me *El Hueso,* the bone. I kind of like it." He ran a hand through his hair and left me sitting on the stool.

I couldn't believe he liked being called El Hueso. Something else I couldn't wrap my brain around was that he'd wet himself and it didn't faze him one way or the other.

The door opened slightly. El Hueso stuck his head in. "About at school the other day: sorry I made fun of you, Miguel."

"Don't do it again, and we're OK."

He smiled and the door closed.

He was right. If he could go out to the store wet like he was, I could be fat and pushing myself home on a buggy or sitting at my own special table at school instead of at a desk for regular-size kids, or ordering super-size clothes from specialty stores online. I could be fatter than fat. Besides, it wasn't like I wasn't doing anything about it. I was trying my best to eat right, to get what exercise I could without hurting myself. I'd keep doing it.

I pushed myself off the stool, took a good breath, and headed out to the store myself.

But life isn't so easy as that; sometimes they're not *just* words, and words *are* like rocks. Sometimes, people can take it too far saying what they're saying, and really it's not what people say that hurts the most, but that they say it without thinking it might hurt. Like we aren't even there.

First thing Monday morning, even before the first bell rang, news about El Hueso's incident had gotten around. Sitting on the benches just outside the library, I heard kids walking past, laughing it up at his expense.

I kept one eye out for him and the other on my watch. A bus pulled up and kids climbed out in a quiet, orderly way. A few of them had grins on their faces and looked over their shoulders occasionally; others made faces like something on the bus stank. As soon as their feet hit the ground, they took off laughing, loud now.

It was ten minutes to the start of class, so I pushed myself up and started walking to English. As I pulled open the door to Hall D, I saw El Hueso get off the bus, his hands shoved deep into his pants pockets, his skinny shoulders sagging, just about the downest-looking guy I've ever seen. And he was headed in the opposite direction. Those fools on the bus had been making fun of him.

I yelled out to him, "Hueso, man. What's up? You lost or what? English is this way."

Without turning, he waved me off.

In class, Roy was telling the story he'd heard from his older sister who works in the pharmacy at H.E.B., who heard it from somebody in produce, who heard it from somebody else in the bakery: "Yeah, so, Tony, right, get this, he peed his pants from his waist to the tips of his shoes. The way I heard it, he was left standing in a puddle of his own urine, right? And he was crying like a baby."

Someone else added, "If he cries like a baby, and he pees on himself like a baby, maybe he needs to be wearing diapers like one, too."

Everyone laughed.

Then they stopped cold. I noticed El Hueso had walked in. He was a completely new person, his shoulders straight, looking up but not into people's eyes. He saw me and nodded a greeting. I nodded back.

I made my way to my table, shaking my head at Roy.

He must've seen me because he said, "Hey, Gordo, why you shaking your head? *Oyes,* you work at the H.E.B., *¿que* no?"

"Yeah," I answered. "So, what of it?" I knew what was coming. His smile said it all. Roy was looking for an ally. He thought I'd be it, because what else does the fat boy want more than anything in this world but to be accepted, to be part of the in group, to finally not be the object of ridicule, even if it means hurting somebody else's feelings?

"So if anyone can tell it right, you can. I heard you were there when it happened."

The others turned to me, waiting for the eyewitness to set the record straight. "Sure, I was there. I know exactly what happened."

Out of the corner of my eye, I saw El Hueso sink into his chair.

In anticipation Roy bared his teeth like a hyena. "So I'm right, right? Tony over there got the pee scared out of him, yeah?" He was laughing. So were some of the others. Our teacher was out getting a refill of coffee in the lounge across the hall before the next bell rang.

"Well? So?" Roy insisted.

"Yeah," some of the others joined in.

I glanced over at Tony, but he was staring straight ahead at the blackboard. I wondered why he wasn't looking back at me. Was he worried I'd forgotten our talk in the locker room at work? How we'd left off as kind of friends? Did he think I was so spineless that I'd do anything, *anything* to get in with Roy and his crowd? Kind of like he'd done?

Honestly, he was right to be concerned. I mean, for once it'd be me pointing a finger at somebody else. "Gordilongo," he'd said to me his first day, "you eat the principal, or what?"

Truth be told, though, I wasn't really tempted. I knew how it worked with clowns like Roy. Today they'd pat me on the back; tomorrow I'd be the laughingstock.

"So?" Roy wanted to know.

"You got no clue, man. No idea whatsoever what happened at work."

"Clear it up for me, then. He'd tell on you like this," he said, and snapped his fingers.

"Maybe, maybe not."

Roy got in my face. "You going to be like that, fatso," he whispered.

I kept quiet.

"You're the one who's got no clue, Gordilongo."

I was tired of this. Of fools like Roy not knowing anything about nothing. I took a step forward.

"Oooh," said Roy. "The giant awakes."

"Leave it alone," I said.

"Or what?" Roy wanted to know.

I took another step. A few more and I'd have him scrunched up against the wall.

Instead, he shoved me and I nearly fell backward, catching myself on a few desks.

Roy charged toward me.

I couldn't right myself because he was towering over me.

"You're nothing but a fat tub of lard," he spat.

No one said a word. Most of the kids inched their ways to their desks. Roy, in their minds most likely, had stepped over a line.

My arms and legs were beginning to tremble. I'd fall to the floor any second now.

"Hey," screamed El Hueso. "Your beef's with me, right?"

Roy turned, a look of disbelief on his face. "What?"

"You heard me, idiot. You want to hear the story? I'll tell it to you. Sure, I wet myself. I wet myself because I've got a big mouth, acting all tough on my first day, and a guy there put the fear of God into me. Sure I wet myself, but I learned something that day. I learned this guy here, Miguel, is more of a man than you'll ever be. And that's no pun."

"Huh? Yeah, well . . ." Roy started.

"Well nothing. You heard what you wanted to hear. Now what? Tell a couple jokes at my expense? Go ahead. Words are just words. I got something better."

René Saldaña Jr.

El Hueso walked up to me, offered his hand. "I got your back, Miguel."

I took his help. It wasn't likely he'd be any real help, but it was the thought that counted. It was action. Talking the talk, walking the walk.

"Call me Gordo, why don't you?"

I don't kid myself. I'm a fat guy. But I got me a good friend now, and he's skinny like a bone.

ABOUT THE AUTHOR AND THE STORY

After teaching middle school and high school and earning a PhD from Georgia State University, René Saldaña Jr. currently teaches in the College of Education at Texas Tech University in Lubbock, where he lives with his wife, Tina, their sons, Lukas and Mikah, and their cat, ISBN. In addition to publishing poems and stories in anthologies, literary journals, and magazines such as *READ* and *Boys' Life,* he is the author of two novels and a book of short stories, all of which celebrate friendships and family life in the barrio. His first novel, *The Jumping Tree,* was a *Booklist* Top Ten Young Adult First Novel and one of New York Public Library's 100 Titles for Reading and Sharing, while his book of short stories, *Finding Our Way,* was a Chicago Public Library Best of the Best Book, a New York Public Library Book for the Teen Age, and a National

Council for the Social Studies Notable Trade Book for Young People. His newest novel is *The Whole Sky Full of Stars*.

Saldaña says that although he is not technically obese, he does struggle with his weight. "I've been steadily losing a couple of pounds here and there, but I'm not truly committed to the idea yet. There's always something that gets in the way: work, taking care of two boys, eating out (fast food is so easy, and worse, I use the drive-through). All of these, though, are nothing more than excuses for me. Excuses because I'm able to lose the weight if I set my mind to it."

Others are not so fortunate, says Saldaña. Like Gordo in this story. Some are not fat by choice but by genetic makeup, though others simply eat too much and exercise too little. The World Health Organization estimates that more than 15 percent of teenagers today are seriously overweight—triple the number of twenty years earlier—with obesity being more common among Mexican-American and African-American teens than among other racial groups. According to KidsHealth.org, obesity in children and teens can lead to typical adult illnesses such as diabetes, high blood pressure, arthritis, liver disease, bladder problems, strokes, certain cancers, depression, and premature death.

"Obese people do what they can," says Saldaña, "to the point of undergoing surgery to correct this problem, but society still looks cross at the FAT. Life is difficult enough without being ostracized. And oftentimes, folks can be so cruel."

Courtney is not who she used to be.
But how long can she hide the truth from everyone?

Brainiac

ALEX FLINN

I'm late to class my first day back because I got lost. That would be OK if I was a freshman, or even a sophomore. But I'm a senior. Seniors are supposed to know where things are. Seniors *do* know where things are. Except me. I thought I knew where my class was, but the whole school got turned around when I wasn't looking.

At least the teacher hasn't started. He's sitting at his desk. I look at the empty seats. There are two, both in a row by the window. One's next to Ty Williams. He's a football player. We were friends last year, because I was a cheerleader. The other is by a girl I don't know. At least, I don't think I know her, a quiet-looking girl with a white polo shirt all buttoned up, and khaki pants.

Ty's waving. "Hey, Court! Over here!"

But I choose the girl. Better to sit by someone who doesn't know how I was before. I start for the seat. Ty's still yelling, "Court-NEE!" I want him to stop. I'm hoping the teacher won't notice I'm late. If he makes me go and get a late pass from my first period teacher, I might never make it back here. That would be hard to explain.

"Courtney!"

I wave to Ty. That's when the teacher notices me. "Nice of you to join us, Miss . . ."

"Evans," I say. "I'm sorry I'm late. I got . . . stuck. There were a lot of people in the hall, and I forgot my locker combination and dropped my books and had to pick them up, and . . ."

I keep going. People start giggling, then laughing, and the whole time, I'm thinking, *Please, don't make me get a pass. Please.*

"Fine." Mr. Davis cuts me off. "Just sit down, please, and sign the seating chart that's coming around."

His face has that look, that polite/mad look people have been getting a lot. Mom says it's because I talk too much now. I try not to, but the problem is, I don't know I'm doing it until I'm already doing it, until they have the look, and it's too late.

"I'm sorry," I say.

"Please sit down."

"Sorry." I sit and look at the girl. I wonder if I *do* know her. She looks a little like this girl I knew in elementary school, whose name was Maria. But I haven't seen her since then. She might go here. I lost track of a lot of people since grade school, because I was always in brainiac honors classes. But since the accident, I'm in regular, where I don't know anyone except Ty.

I look again. She does look like Maria.

I take out my notebook to write down what the teacher says. Mom says I need to write everything down, since my memory's so bad. She also said to try and get phone numbers from two people in each class so I can call if I forget to write something down. I look at the girl. Maria?

"Hi," I say.

She looks at the teacher. Still not talking. "Hi," she whispers.

"My name is Courtney."

"I know who you are. You're a cheerleader, right? Courtney Evans?"

"Yeah, I am. I mean, I'm not a cheerleader anymore, but I'm still Courtney Evans."

Sort of.

"You changed your hair, right? It looks cute."

I run my hand over my ultrashort haircut. It's grown in now, since they shaved it at the hospital. It sort of looks like I cut it this way on purpose. But I didn't.

I remember what I'm supposed to say. "What's your name?"

"Jasmine. Jasmine Hernandez."

I quick write down, *Jasmine. Next to me in language arts.* When I look back over, she's giving my paper a weird look.

"Um . . . bad with names. Writing them helps."

She smiles. "Oh, OK."

"Can I put your phone number, too? We can maybe call each other if we forget the homework."

She smiles bigger. I know why. Courtney Evans, high-school star, asking for her phone number, her friendship. She doesn't know it's the new, brain-damaged Courtney who's doing the asking.

"Sure." She reaches for my notebook, and I have to hand it to her, even though it's full of notes, notes on things normal people don't have to take notes on. Like where my locker is. Like how much lunch costs.

But she doesn't look at that stuff, or at least she doesn't say she does. She just writes her phone number and gives back the notebook. Then she rips a slip of paper from her own notebook and hands it to me.

I stare at it. "What's that for?"

She looks like I threw something at her. "For your phone number."

"Oh . . . sure." I take the paper and write my number, which, thankfully, has been my number since I was born. I have no problem remembering things that happened when I was three, four, five. It's remembering stuff that happened last period that's the problem.

The teacher's finally done with whatever he was

doing. "OK, everyone should have their textbooks out now."

I didn't hear him say anything about textbooks. Did he say that before I got here? I look around. Everyone else's book is out. Not mine. I lean over to my backpack and start looking.

It isn't there. I look again. No, definitely not there.

I lean forward, hoping he won't notice.

He notices.

"Miss Evans, where is your textbook?"

"I forgot to go to my locker. I'm sorry."

"But you said you went to your locker. You told me not five minutes ago that you were late because you went to your locker."

Did I?

"I'm sorry."

"You need to take this class seriously, Miss Evans."

People giggle around me. I say, "Yes, sir." *Serious as brain damage.*

Maria lets me look at her textbook. At the end of class, the teacher announces, "By Thursday, I want you all to visit the library and bring in a book for your independent reading project. You should choose something relevant to your life."

Shit. My notebook is already in my backpack. I'll never remember this without writing it down. But the bell's ringing, and it's too late to unpack again. Maybe I can remember it just until next period.

Book for Thursday. Relevant to my life.
Book for Thursday. Relevant to my life.

"Bye, Maria," I say.

"It's Jasmine."

"I'm sorry." *Jasmine.*

"That's OK. You said you were bad with names."

I spend the rest of the day apologizing. Apologizing for getting lost, for forgetting stuff, for screwing up. Lunch is the worst. A million people say hello and ask if I'm feeling better. I don't know most of them. But I don't know if I really don't know them or if I just forgot. I smile at everyone, just in case, so no one thinks I'm blowing them off.

I sit alone. My old friends are all mad at me for quitting cheer. Mom wouldn't let me tell them that it was because I had brain damage and couldn't fly or do pyramids anymore. She's worried that the school might not let me stay if they know. So my friends just think I quit because I quit. So they hate me.

Finally, the first day is over. It's easy to find my way outside because everyone's going the same way. Mom picks me up. I can't drive anymore.

"How was it?" she asks.

"I can't do this."

She starts the car, telling me of course I can, telling me all the things that even with my crummy memory I know she's told me a hundred other times: That I just have to get through this one year. Get Ds in everything. Just graduate. If I can do that, Dad will get me a nice job answering phones at one of his friends' law firms, a nice stupid-girl job I can do until I die.

The problem is, I am not stupid. At least, I remember when I wasn't. I used to be Courtney Evans, honors student. Courtney Evans, cheerleader. Courtney Evans, who was going to be a lawyer someday, not a receptionist at a law firm. That Courtney used to look down on people who were stupid and ditzy, the way I am now.

"Want a snack before homework?" At home Mom's trying to sound like the cheery supermom of the cheery superdaughter—the one she used to be.

"I need a nap."

"Courtney, we really need to get started. This could take—"

"I need a nap." I walk to my room and close the door.

But when I get there, I start flipping through my yearbook to the pictures of the junior class, my class, my old friends. Paige. Ashley. Brittanee. It's not fair. They all partied as much as I did. They all got drunk off their asses, and nothing ever happened to them. I wasn't even drunk that night. We'd all signed those stupid pledge things, saying we wouldn't drive drunk, that we'd call Mom or Dad if we needed a ride, that we'd choose a designated driver.

But the guy driving the car that hit me hadn't signed one. And now he's dead and I might as well be. Life as I knew it was over the moment I felt my head hit the side window, when he ran a stop sign and plowed into me.

The other guy was lucky. They hadn't saved him. They saved me, mostly, and I spent the whole summer learning to do things again, learning to walk, to talk. I wonder if Mom started another baby book, with my first word and first steps. But some things, like remembering names of people I just met, like remembering homework, like driving or riding my bike or cheerleading, will always be hard. Mom says I'm still getting better. But I know I'll never be all right again.

Once, before the accident, I saw this Adam Sandler movie, where this girl was in a car accident and suffered short-term memory loss. Every day, she'd wake up and forget what had happened in the days since the accident. It was like time never moved on for her. She just started new every day like it was the day of the accident. That's what I thought they meant by a brain injury.

But what it really means is just being stupid, stupid and forgetful, the way my grandmother is forgetful when she calls me by my mom's name. I'm old-lady forgetful at seventeen.

And the worst thing is, I remember everything about the way I was before.

My mom knocks on the door. I try to quick get into bed and shove everything under the covers, but she opens the door and catches me.

"Courtney. Homework. Now."

"I need to rest. You don't know how hard it is."

"I do know."

"How could you? You're not trying to go to school with half your brain missing."

"It's just one year. Just pass your classes with Ds, and—"

"I don't want to be a receptionist!" I scream. "Don't you understand that?

"Courtney . . ." Her voice is soothing, like she's talking to a baby. "Homework is important."

I sigh, real loud, like that proves my point. But I know she's right. If I can't even manage homework, I'll never be able to do what I want to do.

"Fine," I say, even though my head hurts.

"Good girl." Mom pats my shoulder and reaches for my backpack. I'd never have let her near it before. Before. She takes out my agenda book and checks it.

"You only have homework in math, Courtney?"

I shrug. "Is that what it says?"

"That's the only subject you wrote homework down in. Do you have homework in any other subject?"

I stare ahead, trying to remember.

"Do you have homework in economics?"

I try to picture my economics class. The blackboard. Did it have anything written on it? I don't think so. Wouldn't I have written it down if there was homework?

"I don't think so."

"How about language arts?"

I try again. I feel like maybe there *was* homework in language arts. But why didn't I write it down?

Because you're stupid, that's why.

"I can't remember."

Mom sighs. "You wrote down a girl's name here. Jasmine. It says she sits by you in language arts. Do you want to call her?"

Do I want to? Do I want to explain that I'm a total moron? I feel tears heating up my eyes. "No! She'll think I'm totally stupid. She'll think there's something wrong with me. She'll *know* there is."

"She won't, Courtney." Mom's looking all super-sympathetic. "Baby, you have to call her. You need to do homework. I can help you with that. It might make a difference if you fail at tests."

"Fine!" I say it too loud.

But Mom's already dialing. She hands the phone to me.

"Hi, may I please speak to"— I stop, and Mom points to the name—"Jasmine?"

"This is her. Who's this?"

"It's Courtney. . . . We're in . . . um . . ."

"Language arts," Mom whispers.

"Language arts." I need to talk quick, so I won't think about how dumb I am and stop. "I forgot to write down the homework, and I wonder if you have it."

There's no answer.

"Hello?" I say.

"You have to be kidding," she says finally in a real mad voice. "You blew me off in the cafeteria and about five times today—"

"I did?"

"And now you call, asking a *favor*? Why don't you get the homework from one of your snobby cheer-girl friends?"

"They're not in the class."

"What?"

"That's not what I meant. I mean, I didn't mean to . . . to not say hello. I didn't see—"

"Five times? And you looked right at me."

"You have to believe me." I glance at Mom for help.

"It's confusing the first day," she whispers.

I repeat it and add, "You have to believe me. I don't mean to be snobby."

I'm just stupid.

Finally, she tells me the assignment, a grammar workbook page. I thank her and say I'll see her tomorrow. I hopehopehope I remember to say hello.

Mom helps me with the grammar and the math. They're both pretty easy because I did it last year, then switched to easier classes this year. Even writing essays will be easy, as long as I keep going back and looking at what I already wrote. The hard subjects will be science and economics because they have memorizing stuff. Someone with my memory can't cram for a test. I'll have to study enough to make it really part of my long-term memory,

Dr. Rea says. He also said that people with brain damage can learn new things, and then not even remember that they know them.

It will suck when we start reading books for language arts.

I remember something, something about a book for language arts. A book to buy, maybe? I'm not sure. The teacher usually gives a lot of notice of that stuff, though.

It takes until seven to finish the easy homework in two classes. As soon as I do, I go to bed. I fall asleep, memorizing, *Jasmine. Jasmine. Jasmine.*

The next day, I find second period OK. Mom got a school map and wrote directions in different color pens. I love her for that, but I hate her, too. It would be easier if she just gave up. She must be so disappointed, having a retard daughter.

So when I get to class, it's early. *Too* early. Too many desks are empty. I don't remember where I sit.

"Courtney!"

It's Tyler Williams. I walk over to him, just for something to do. "Hey, how's it going?" I say, trying to act normal. Do I look normal, or can people tell by looking at me that something is very, very wrong?

"How's it going?" I say.

"Good. You feeling all right? I heard about your accident. Sorry I didn't get over to visit."

"That's OK." I look around.

"Something wrong?"

"No." I look around some more. "It's just . . . I forgot where I'm supposed to sit." I hope he doesn't think— know—I'm stupid.

He laughs, but not in a mean way. "You sit by me."

"I do?" Relieved, I take the seat by him and start getting out my books.

"Listen," he says. "I know people have been weird about you quitting the squad and all, but you should come out with us. Andy Duncan's having a party Saturday. We could go together, maybe."

Unbelievable. He's asking me out. If he knew the truth, he never would. Still, Tyler's hardly a rocket scientist. I'd never have liked him before. Maybe . . .

The teacher (whose name I don't even remember!) is telling everyone to get in their seats now. He's taking roll, his eyes going from the rows of seats to his seating chart. They stop on me.

"Where are you supposed to be?"

"Huh?"

"I have that down as an empty seat. You're in the wrong seat."

I stare at him.

"Are you new?"

"I, uh . . . don't think so."

People are giggling all around. I would have, too— before. Stupid people are funny.

"What is your name?"

Finally! A question I can answer. "Courtney Evans."

He checks his chart, frowning, and points to a seat two rows behind me. "Stay in your assigned seat."

"Yeah." I pick up my books, quietly dying, and go to the seat he's pointing at. I wonder if anyone would notice if I wrote, *This one!* in big Sharpie letters on the desk.

I see a girl next to me who looks familiar. She must be the one whose name I spent the night memorizing. Ja . . . Ja . . .

"Hi, Jaime." I give her a big smile.

"It's Jasmine." She doesn't smile back.

I settle for writing my initials in Sharpie on the top left side of the desk.

I hope I'll remember I did it.

The classwork is easy-peasy grammar stuff I can do — yes! — even with brain damage. This is good. Rack up a few As.

I remember to write down my homework.

On the way out, Tyler says, "So, how about it?"

It takes me a second to remember. The party. Andy Duncan.

"I have to ask my mom."

I will, too. Tyler's nice. He's not smart either, so maybe he won't notice how dumb I am now.

*   *   *

That night, I do my homework. We have a chemistry test tomorrow. I used to be good at science, but now it's hard to memorize all the terms. Still, I make flash cards and go over them, like, a million times until I really, really know them, the way I know my own name.

I go through the whole set of fifty flash cards. I feel great! I can do this!

It's really important to be good at science.

What I haven't told Mom, haven't told anyone because it would be just too embarrassing, is that not only do I not want to be a receptionist; what I really want is to be a nurse.

Right.

I figured this out in the hospital, after the accident. My head hurt. I couldn't remember the faces of all the people who came in to look at me, stick me with needles, change bandages. Much less remember their names. But the nurses were all so nice. They didn't care that I was stupid. Once (maybe more than once), I apologized to this one nurse who acted like she knew me, even though I was sure I'd never seen her before.

"How many times have you been in here?" I asked.

"Every day the past week."

"I . . . shit, I'm so screwed. I'm sorry."

"A few times, you were sleeping."

"Still. I should remember you."

She put down the chart she was holding and patted my hand. Then she said, "I've seen a lot worse than you."

"Right."

"No, really. You're doing better than lots of folks I see. At least you know you don't remember. And you'll get better as time goes on."

I had her write her name before she left. It was Delia. And after she went, I wrote down what she looked like. Then, I had *all* the nurses write their names. That was when I started writing everything down. I started looking at the nurses and doctors, and in a few days, I knew them all. But I also knew they were nice to me even when I didn't know.

Nurses can remember all their patients because there are charts on the beds, with patient information hanging on them. They can look stuff up. Some nurses help in surgery, and they need to have four-year degrees (I wrote that down, too), but other nurses only have to go two years.

If I could get through two years of community college, even if it took longer than two years, I could be a nurse.

And today, with my science all memorized, I feel like I can do it.

Wednesday, everything sucks again. I get lost going to almost every class. I forget my book twice. When I see Tyler in language arts, he asks me if I asked my mom.

I say, "Asked her what?"

And I think I failed my chem test, the one I totally studied for and knew.

I was stupid to think I could be a nurse. I'll be lucky if I can work at McDonald's and spend my life having people yell at me for giving them fries when they ordered onion rings.

The only good thing I do is, I remember Jasmine. After I finish talking to Tyler, I walk to my desk and smile. "Hi, Jasmine."

"Whatever," she says back.

That night, Mom comes in to nag me about homework. I tell her, "I can't do this. I need to go to some kind of a special school for stupid people."

"There aren't any schools like that for you, just alternative schools for people who can't handle regular school."

"That's what I *am*!"

"These aren't kids who were in car accidents. They're bad kids, kids with problems. I couldn't send my daughter to a school like that, especially a girl like . . ." She stops.

"A girl like what?"

"A girl like you, one who's . . ."

"Stupid?"

"Vulnerable."

"God, I'm a total retard."

"Just get Ds, honey—D is for Diploma. Get a D in everything, and you'll—"

"I know. I'll graduate and get a nice job answering phones."

I open my notebook for my homework assignments. I forgot to write them down.

Perfect.

Thursday, I don't have the homework in any of my classes. In language arts, Mr. Davis asks for the book we brought.

"What book?" I say to Jasmine.

She doesn't even answer. I turn to the guy behind me. "What book?"

"The book for your independent reading project. Something *relevant to your life.*" He makes quote marks with his fingers.

I start to write that down when Mr. Davis says, "Miss Evans, what book did you bring?"

"Sorry. I forgot."

He actually leaves his desk and walks all the way over to mine. "Miss Evans, you're obviously a smart girl."

"No, I'm not," I say, and people giggle.

"I've seen your test scores. I know you were in AP classes. But this year, you're nothing but trouble, forgetting materials, not doing homework. Is this all a big joke to you?"

"No, sir."

He backs away. "That's an F for the day, and every day you don't bring it from now on."

I put my head on my desk. The boy who sits in front of me and doesn't speak to me laughs. "Serves her right, snotty bitch."

Friday is a repeat of Thursday. Fifty-nine percent on my chemistry test. The teacher sends it home for Mom to sign and suggests a parent-teacher conference.

Great. Maybe he'll say I'm too stupid to go here.

But I want to go to school. I want to graduate. I don't want my whole life to be over at seventeen.

Maybe it would have been better if I'd died in the accident. At least people would remember me as being smart.

My economics teacher gives us a list of terms to memorize for a test next Thursday.

I get another F in language arts. Mr. Davis gives me a note for Mom. *Despite her obvious abilities, Courtney is in serious danger of failing.*

I show the notes to Mom.

"Try harder," she says.

Friday night, I know my friends are all at Andy's party, talking about what a snob I've gotten to be. Is that better or worse than thinking—knowing—I'm stupid?

* * *

Monday comes. No book.

"I don't understand it, Miss Evans." Mr. Davis marks another F in his gradebook. "Your teachers from last year all say you were an ideal student. I've heard of senioritis, but this. . . . Don't you care if you fail my class?"

Everyone's staring. A few people laugh, especially Tyler. Mr. Davis starts to walk away. He isn't expecting an answer to his question.

But I want to answer. I'm so far gone already that there's nothing to lose if I answer. Most people would get all defiant to show they don't care, but I say, "I do care."

He turns. "I don't have time for this. Everyone, take your books out."

"You don't have time?" I stand up and scream it, and the standing up is so sudden, so hard, that I almost fall back down. I put my hands in front of me. "Is that what you said?"

"Miss Evans, sit down."

"No!" People are whispering, giggling, and I say, "No, you don't understand. I want to do better, but this is the best I can do, the best I can do now. I'm not the same as I used to be." I know I have to say the words. "I have brain damage."

"Sit down, Miss . . ." His voice trails off. "What?"

"My brain doesn't work right. I had an accident, and now I can do some things, like diagramming sentences, or writing essays, or math, but I can't do other things, easy things like remembering the person who sits next to me or remembering to bring a book if I don't write it down. I'm *stupid. Stupid.* My mom says not to tell anyone, because they'll think I'm too stupid to go to this school. But maybe I am. I feel stupid all the time. I don't want to be someone people feel sorry for, but I can't do this. I can't do this."

I'm crying now, and I run out of the room as fast as I can without running into something. I go to the bathroom and stay until third period.

After lunch, my fifth period teacher hands me a note. It says to go back to Mr. Davis's class after school. "Can you remember that?" Mrs. Cirrone says, so I know she knows. They all know.

"I'll write it on my hand," I say.

When I get to Davis's class, all my teachers are there, and so is my mother. "I'm sorry," I tell her. "I screwed up."

She smiles. "Maybe I screwed up. Sometimes you need a little help."

Mr. Davis is running the meeting, and he starts talking. I don't understand all he says, but I get a lot of it. Help writing down homework. Extra time for memorization tests. He says they'll have to talk to my doctors and the school psychologist.

"Courtney," he says, "we want you to succeed. You've been very brave, but you don't have to do it alone."

And that's when I start crying again, so I don't really get anything else.

When I'm leaving with my mother, I remember something. "I'll bring the book tomorrow," I say. "My mom's here, so I'll get her to take me to buy it."

"Oh, don't worry about that," Mr. Davis says. "I have the perfect one in mind. I'll bring it tomorrow."

I nod. Must be some book about some stupid person who made it, against all odds. I know how language arts teachers are about books. But for the first time since school started, I don't feel like I'm drowning.

When I get to language arts the next day, Jasmine smiles. "Courtney, I'm Jasmine."

"I know," I say. "I finally memorized you."

"That's great." She hands me a sheet of notebook paper. "I wrote down your homework for you. I told Mr. Davis I'd do it every day."

I can't even thank her. I sit at my desk, which still has my initials on it. There's a book on top of it, too. The title is *Hatchet* by some guy named Gary Paulsen.

I raise my hand. "Yes, Courtney?" Mr. Davis is all smiles.

"Someone forgot this book here," I say.

"I left it for you. It's for your project. I know it might be a little below your reading level, but it seemed appropriate anyway."

"Oh. Thanks." I turn the book over to look at the back. It says it's about a boy who is lost in the Canadian wilderness when his plane crashes. He has nothing but a hatchet. It looks easy, too easy. I can read, after all.

I raise my hand again. "But I thought . . . it's . . . something . . . you said . . . relevant, right?" When Mr. Davis nods, I go on. "But it's about an airplane crash . . . wilderness . . . a hatchet. I'm not even sure what a hatchet is. How is that . . . ?"

Mr. Davis leaves his desk and walks toward me. He puts his hand on my shoulder. People have been doing that a lot since yesterday. Then he points to the book. "This book is just like you," he says.

"How?"

"You're both survival stories."

I look at the book cover, Mr. Davis's face, Jasmine's neatly printed notes, and I know he's right.

I'll survive.

ABOUT THE AUTHOR AND THE STORY

Alex Flinn established a high standard of writing for herself with her first novel, *Breathing Underwater,* an unflinching story about a teenage boy who has been arrested for being physically abusive to his girlfriend. That novel earned numerous accolades, including an American Library Association Top Ten Books for

Young Adults selection, an ALA Quick Pick, and a Black-Eyed Susan Book Award. The Young Adult Library Services Association also chose it as one of the 100 Best of the Best for the 21st Century, 1994–2003. That book was followed by *Breaking Point, Nothing to Lose,* and *Fade to Black,* each of which earned significant honors, including being chosen as an ALA Best Book for Young Adults, an ALA Quick Pick, a *Booklist* Top Ten Youth Mystery, and nominations to young adult book lists in more than a dozen states.

In most recent novel *Diva,* Flinn examines the life of Caitlin, the abused girlfriend in *Breathing Underwater,* as she tries to get on with her life by switching to a performing arts school and focusing on her opera singing talent while coming to terms with her mother's dating behaviors. Alex Flinn is also the author of two other novels: *A Kiss in Time,* which is a retelling of "Sleeping Beauty," and *Beastly,* a retelling of "Beauty and Beast," which has been made into a feature film.

Her previously published short stories appear in *Destination Unexpected; Rush Hour: A Journal of Contemporary Voices, Vol. 1: Sin;* and *Twice Told: Eighteen Original Stories Inspired by Original Art,* and one of her stories is the lead selection in *What Are You Afraid Of? Stories About Phobias.*

Brain damage, Alex Flinn explains, became the basis for this story because her daughter has a friend whose mother suffers from this disability as a result of brain surgery when she was a teenager. "This woman," Flinn says, "once mentioned to me that she attended college following the surgery, and I remember thinking how difficult that must have been, and how determined she must have been to do it because she really is seriously forgetful, while still having the ability to do many things. I have always found her perseverance admirable and wanted to write a story about a character like her, a survivor."

Flinn's research on brain damage, including the difference between long- and short-term memory stores, and different forms of amnesia that can be caused by brain injury, revealed how brain-injured people like Courtney can learn.

*Cancer can kill you, but
you don't have to kiss its butt.*

Let's Hear It for Fire Team Bravo

ROBERT LIPSYTE

Eddie didn't look at me when I showed up in our hospital room. He was sitting up in bed, clutching his pillow to his bony chest, staring at the little TV hanging from the ceiling.

Nurse Laurel said, "Eddie, say hello to your new roommate, Michael."

Maybe he mumbled something, but I didn't hear it. I wasn't hearing much that day. I was hot and cold. My tongue stuck to the top of my mouth. Scared spitless.

Eddie had long hair hanging over a pale, pimply face. He looked about fifteen, but he had to be at least two years older, my age, or he'd be downstairs in Pediatrics. I don't think his eyes ever left the screen.

Dad put my backpack on my bed and looked out the window at the brick wall across the hospital courtyard. Really studied it. He'd been having trouble looking at me. Mom zipped open the backpack and started taking out my laptop. "We'll be expecting your IMs and texts all day long, and I know your friends will—"

"Didn't admissions tell you?" Nurse Laurel sounded annoyed. "No laptops. Cells are prohibited. . . ."

"We're prisoners," said Eddie in a high, scratchy voice. "On death row."

Mom said, "Is this the only room available?"

Nurse Laurel poked into the backpack, took out my iPod and my slippers and handed the backpack to Dad. "Give me a chance to get Michael settled." She started herding them out the door, but Mom broke loose to give me a long, hard hug. Dad said something I didn't hear. Then they were gone. If Nurse Laurel hadn't blocked the way, I would have run out after them. She handed me a blue hospital gown. "Wear it open in the back."

I got into bed and plugged myself into my iPod. I didn't notice the two young doctors until they were at my bed, grinning at me.

"I'm Dr. Wong." She pointed to a rumpled guy who also wore a white coat and stethoscope. "This is Dr. Krajic. We're Urology Fellows."

"They're like students," said Eddie. "They don't know squat."

They scraped little plastic chairs up to the bed and opened notebooks. "So when did you first notice the mass on your testicle?" said Dr. Krajic.

I felt weird talking in front of Dr. Wong. "I already told a lot of doctors. . . ."

"They're like cops," said Eddie. "They want to see if you change your story so they can fry your ass."

"I'm the good cop," said Dr. Krajic, laughing.

"We need to take a history," said Dr. Wong. "You do want to get better, don't you?"

I didn't want them to get mad at me, so I said, "I just felt it. Like a pea. It was sore."

"How long between your first noticing the mass, Michael, and your coming here?" asked Dr. Wong.

"I don't know—a couple of months."

They looked at each other. What did that mean? I was going to die? "Am I going to die?"

"Testicular cancer has over a ninety percent cure rate," said Dr. Wong.

"Unless you're one of the ten percent," said Eddie.

"Lance Armstrong had it in his brain," said Dr. Wong, "and he went on to win the Tour de France seven times."

"We only expect you to win once," said Dr. Krajic. He cracked up and high-fived Dr. Wong.

Eddie just snorted and turned back to the TV.

I went through the whole story about going to my family doctor, who told me to take hot baths to make the pea go away, which it didn't, and then to the local urologist, who was excited because he hardly ever saw testicular cancer, and then Mom remembered an old boyfriend who was a big-deal cancer doc, and she called him . . .

"Dr. Kenny," said Dr. Wong, "is a god around here."

. . . and he saw me the next morning and felt the pea and put me in the hospital that afternoon. This afternoon.

"You are sooo lucky," said Dr. Wong.

"If you were sooo lucky, you wouldn't be here," said Eddie.

"What's going to happen?" I croaked.

"Tomorrow, Dr. Kenny will take a look, and depending on what he sees, that's what will happen next."

"Which is?" I said.

"Let's not get ahead of ourselves," said Dr. Wong as she stood up.

As they walked out, Dr. Krajic said, "We'll see."

Eddie said, *"Now a bobbing speck on the Will Sea."*

"Sounds like poetry," I said.

"You like poetry?" He looked interested.

I hated poetry. I didn't understand it. I thought people who said they did were either fakers or people who looked down on me or both. But I was such a wimp. I didn't want people mad at me.

"Poetry's cool," I said.

Eddie looked hard at me, to see if I was mocking him. "You want to know what happens next? Tomorrow, they cut you open and take out your ball on a string, and if it's nothing, which it never is, they put your ball back and send you home. If it is something, which it always is, they chop you up some more, and then they blast poison through your body."

"Is that what they did to you?"

"Not anymore," he said. *"Wouldn't beach on their sun-broiled sand / Dance hot-footed to their tunes."*

That sounded familiar but I couldn't remember where I had heard it. Maybe the show *Dancing with the Survivors.* While I tried to remember, Eddie turned up the volume on his TV, and that was the last he talked to me that night. Dinner arrived, gray mystery meat and green mystery veggies. I ate the yellow mystery ice cream.

Lights started dimming in the hallway when a lean guy in jeans and a Marine T-shirt swaggered in. Shaven skull, sharp jaw, piercing blue eyes. A video-game face. Just the kind of jock bully who looks down on you.

"Welcome to Fire Team Bravo," he said. He stuck out a hand to shake. It was gentler than I imagined. He pumped my arm. "I'm Sergeant Whip, your team leader."

"What?"

"Team means you're not alone, brothers got your back. All you need to know for now is that cancer can kill you, but you don't have to kiss its butt. What's your name?"

"Michael."

"We'll fix that." He pumped my arm again. "We'll take you down tomorrow for your orchiectomy. It's a walk in the park."

"Wait," I said as he turned to leave. "Eddie says they cut you open and take out your ball on a string, and if it's nothing, which it never is, they put your ball back and send you home. If it is something, which it always is, they chop you up some more, and then they blast poison through your body."

"That's the soft, scared, head-in-the-sand negative way of looking at it," he said crisply. "The Fire Team Bravo way is to identify the enemy, shoot it to death, then burn what's left. See you in the a.m."

He glanced over his shoulder. "Get with the program, Maverick."

Eddie mumbled something that sounded like *"not your type."*

When Sergeant Whip was gone, I said, "What was that all about?"

Eddie said, *"I sing in italics,"* then turned up the TV and disappeared back into the screen.

* * *

They came for me before breakfast. Injections, exams, and then I was out in the hall being pushed by Nurse Laurel. Shadowy figures came out of rooms and walked alongside my rolling bed. Sergeant Whip had his hand on my shoulder. "Duke's here. Bugs, Rocket, Tank. Predator's getting a port put in and Lobo's in ICU. Fire Team Bravo's got your back, Michael.

Michael?" said one of the shadows. "What kind of name's that?"

"We'll fix it," said Sergeant Whip.

I woke up cold in a room filled with bodies. Other dead bodies, I thought, until I saw some of them waking up, too. After a long time, they wheeled me back into my room. Before I fell asleep, I thought I saw Sergeant Whip giving me the thumbs-up.

Mom was crying and Dad was studying the brick wall, and Dr. Kenny was looking at me down there. "Good scar. In a year you'll never see it again."

"When will you do it?" said Mom.

"End of the week when all the tests are in and Martin—"

"Michael."

"—is feeling strong. It's an eight-hour operation; we'll be looking for cells."

All I could think of was that cells were prohibited. Also laptops.

"And then?"

"We'll see."

The Will Sea again. I felt like I was drowning.

My head didn't clear until the next morning. Sergeant Whip came in with a big fat guy he introduced as Tank and a jittery little guy he called Bugs.

"So what you got?" said Bugs.

"Cancer," I said.

"Duh," said Bugs. "I'm here for a nose job."

"I'm here for a butt lift," said Tank.

"How high?" said Bugs.

"So your momma can reach it," said Tank.

"The questions are," said Whip, "what stage cancer, what kind of cell, has it broken through?"

My throat closed up. "I don't know," I said.

"You need to know, need to get involved. Intel, recon, engagement. There's a Fire Team meeting tonight after dinner. My room."

"I just had an operation," I said. "An orchiectomy."

"We all had those," said Whip.

"No sex for twenty-four hours," said Tank.

"Unless Tank's sister shows up again," said Bugs.

"Enough," snapped Whip. He jabbed a finger at me. "Be at the meeting. You, too, Maverick."

"Because you say so?" said Eddie.

"I understand you've got authority issues," said Whip. "Don't let them get in the way of your survival."

"You're an authority?" sneered Eddie. "What? Tennessee Valley Authority? Port Authority? Palestinian Authority?"

"I like that," said Sergeant Whip. "You're fighting back, Maverick, even if you've got the wrong target."

"Don't call me Maverick. *I'm no boldface name / No lowercase cutie.*"

Whip rolled his eyes and signaled Tank and Bugs. They all marched out of the room.

When they were gone, I said to Eddie, "What's going on?"

"They're living in a fantasy, a video game." He pulled the curtain around his bed.

I was wheeled around the hospital for tests. I was slid through a humming machine while a mechanical voice told me to take a deep breath, hold it, breathe. A hundred times.

When I asked her what was going on, a woman explained that they were scanning my organs.

Later, a needle was stuck into my foot and dye was shot into my veins. I watched on TV. It didn't hurt much and it was interesting. When I asked what was going on, a guy said they were tracking hot spots.

*   *   *

At the meeting that night, Sergeant Whip had me report on my day. One guy said, "Scanning for what? And what are hot spots?"

"Nightclubs with good drugs," said Bugs.

Everybody laughed. At me.

I was sorry I had gone to the meeting, but I'd felt lonely after Mom and Dad left. My sister, Kerri, had flown home from college in Michigan, a big deal, which I appreciated, but it scared me. Did she think I was in deep trouble? When her fingers dug into my arm and she told me, "We'll get you through this, Mikey," I had to bite the inside of my cheek not to cry. Then the doctors came in. Dr. Kenny and the Fellows whispered among themselves, "We'll see, Will Sea," and I was underwater.

Eddie wouldn't talk to me. He was talking to his pillow.

So I had gone to the room Sergeant Whip shared with Tank. Whip was sitting in a lounge chair, a needle in his arm, running the meeting. Tank and Bugs stood on each side of him, arms crossed, like guards. The three other guys introduced themselves—Duke and Rocket and Predator. They were kind of a blur. Everything was a blur.

"OK, what's the schedule?" said Whip.

One by one, each of the guys listed what was going on in his treatment. Predator was starting chemo. Rocket was waiting for an operation. Guys that had been through it offered tips.

"Get your painkillers started before you feel too much pain," said Tank.

"That's good," said Whip. "Stay ahead of the hurt. OK, Michael. Ready for your RND?"

"What?"

"Brief him, Duke," said Sergeant Whip.

"The retroperitoneal node dissection," said Duke, "is the big recon operation. The good guys go in there looking for bad guys, mark the targets so they can call in air strikes."

"Excellent," said Whip. "Duke's Intel."

"Intel?" I said.

"Intelligence chief."

I just stood there. What was he talking about? "This sounds like a video game."

"Gotta get him out of that room," said Bugs.

"Listen up, Michael," said Whip. "This is a war. We're in combat. Cancer cells can ambush you, leave land mines. You need to fight as a group."

"Michael?" said Tank. "That's no name for a fighter."

"Need to get it right this time," said Whip. "Don't want to make another mistake."

"Don't get down on yourself," said Duke. "Cut the punk loose."

"I haven't given up on Maverick yet," said Whip. "Fire Teams don't leave their wounded behind."

*　　*　　*

Eddie was out of the room when Dr. Wong and Dr. Krajic came to see me the next morning.

"Anything you'd like to talk about, Michael?"

There were a lot of things I wanted to talk about, like hair falling out and would I be able to have sex, but I didn't feel comfortable talking to her. So I said, "What's with Eddie?"

They looked at each other. "Do you want to be moved?" said Dr. Wong.

I thought about it. I could end up with Whip or Bugs. Maybe this wasn't so bad. "No, I just wondered."

"We can't talk about another patient," said Dr. Wong.

"We can't tell you he's making a big mistake," said Dr. Krajic.

"After all Dr. Kenny has done for him. Saved his life. Given him a chance."

They left shaking their heads.

I went to see Intel. He was getting chemo in his bed. It was bubbling out of plastic bags hanging from metal stands, down through tubes into his veins.

"Word is," said Duke, "if Eddie won't go back on chemo, they'll discharge him."

"Then what happens?"

"If he doesn't fight back," said Duke, "he's gone. Six months, a year. It's in his lungs and liver."

* * *

Eddie had visitors, his family, I figured, but they always closed the curtain around his bed and argued with him. I thought about him a lot. That way I didn't have to think about me. The RND. Chemo. Will Sea.

When I had visitors, mostly Mom, Dad, and Kerri that first week, I took them out to the visitors' room on the floor or upstairs to the nice lounge on the roof.

"Why'd you name him Maverick?" I asked Whip.

"I thought he was a rebel," said Whip. "But he wimped."

"Quit chemo," said Bugs. "We're done with him."

"Bad for morale," said Predator.

"Predator's the morale chief," said Whip. "He gets us DVDs, arranges text messages, under the radar, of course. Need anything?"

"I thought," I said, "Fire Teams never leave their wounded behind."

Whip looked at me sharply. "That's good. You're getting with the program. I think you might have moxie. But I've decided he's not wounded. He's going AWOL. He's bailing out on the Fire Team."

"Maybe he's got a right to make his own decision with his own life," I said. Why was I defending Eddie?

"In combat, you can't have a guy you can't depend on,

who thinks he's dancing to some different music than everybody else." Suddenly, Whip seemed very tired. "OK, let's move on to the schedule. Lobo?"

It came to me in the middle of that night. Eddie was moaning in his sleep, and I thought of Whip saying, "In combat, you can't have a guy you can't depend on, who thinks he's dancing to some different music than everybody else." That made me remember something Eddie had said. *Dance hot-footed to their tunes.* It wasn't from a TV show. It was from a poem we had to read in English. Dumb poem. Didn't understand it.

They kept me busier the closer we got to the Big Op, the retroperitoneal node dissection. They kept wheeling me around to more tests, X-rays, visits with other doctors, some of them shrinks who asked me how I felt. I asked them about hair and sex. They said it affected different people differently. We'll see. Will Sea.

Dr. Kenny was always too busy to answer questions about the RND, and Dr. Wong and Dr. Krajic didn't really know the answers. So I asked Kerri to go online for me. And not to tell Mom and Dad.

I also asked her to bring my *Modern American Poetry* textbook. She raised an eyebrow at that. She knew how I felt about poetry. I asked her to bring it wrapped in the cover of my history textbook. And find out what the word *moxie* meant. Without my laptop and cell, I felt like I was on a desert island.

Fire Team Bravo walked me to the RND. I figured my eyes were loose in my head, because Sergeant Whip seemed wobbly, hanging on to my rolling bed for support. His voice was hoarse, whispery.

"Remember, cancer can kill you, but you don't have to kiss its butt," he said. "Stay tough."

"Kill cancer," said Lobo, tapping my leg through the blanket.

They all chanted, "Kill cancer," and tapped me through the blanket before I went through the big doors to the Operating Suites. Really dumb, I thought, and I was glad they were there.

I woke up again in cold hell in a room of bodies. If I wasn't dead, I thought, I was in a scene from *CSI*.

CSI Siberia?

Then they wheeled me to a warmer room with fewer bodies. *CSI Baghdad.*

When I got back to my room, Kerri whispered that the stuff I had asked for was stashed in my locker.

Whip was in a wheelchair. "You made it, troop," he said.

"Better believe it, Sarge," I said.

"Outstanding."

This time, it took days for my head to clear. I have only out-of-focus snapshots of those days. In one, Dr. Kenny peeled back bandages that covered most of my front side. "Good scar."

"Will it be gone in a year?" asked Mom.

"He'll always have a good scar," said Dr. Kenny.

"What's next?" asked Dad.

"After all the test results are in, the oncologists will figure out what kind of chemo Michael needs."

Eddie said, "Welcome to nausea, vomiting, hair loss, mouth sores, phantom foot and hand pains, kidney failure."

Dr. Kenny pulled the curtain closed around my bed. "He won't be here much longer," he said.

I think I said, "We'll see," but maybe I only thought it.

I was in a lot of pain from the Big Op, so I was drugged for days. It was a while before I got to the intel Kerri had stashed in my locker.

It was just what I needed. I found out what *moxie* meant: Gutsy and smart, especially in tough times.

I could live with that.

And I found the poem.

*　*　*

The TV was on over Eddie's bed.

"Eddie," I said. "You awake?"

He said something like, "No, I'm asleep."

I said, *"Let's hear it for Big Boy G / Stroking toward the horizon."*

He said, "They sent you to spy on me." But he didn't pull the curtain.

"Wouldn't beach on their sun-broiled sand / Dance hot-footed to their tunes. Like you."

"Okay, big deal, so you read a poem. That doesn't mean you know anything."

"Now a bobbing speck on the Will Sea."

Then I pulled my curtain shut. I had him muttering to himself. I didn't want to spoil it by letting him find out that I had just used up all the poetry I had memorized. Those lines were from the next-to-last stanza of a poem called "Five Prescriptions" by a poet named B. B. Goings. I hadn't understood his stuff. The teacher and the kids who claimed they understood poetry said that B. B. was an e. e. cummings wannabe. I hadn't understood that guy's stuff either.

Maybe you have to be in the mood. After I read B. B.'s poem five or six times in the lounge on the roof, it began to make some sense.

Robert Lipsyte

FIVE PRESCRIPTIONS
by B. B. Goings

I sing in italics because
I'm no boldface name
No lowercase cutie
No uppercase screamer
Not your type

Sick is sick
No test
No punishment
Not the pre-season
For Better Days

Some things are worse
Than death
But until you've tried them
After death
Who knows?

Let's hear it for Big Boy G
Stroking toward the horizon
Wouldn't beach on their sun-broiled sand
Dance hot-footed to their tunes
Now a bobbing speck on the Will Sea

Superman lent me his cape
Didn't fit
Had to weave my own
From steely dreams
Here I come

At the next Fire Team meeting, I gave a sex report right out of what Kerri had gotten off the Internet from a medical site. She had a friend who was pre-med.

"Sex is different after the RND," I said, sounding as tough as I could, "so you virgins are never gonna know the difference."

I waited for the laughs to die down. Sergeant Whip was sitting up in bed, nodding me on. He'd lost weight and his eyes were feverish.

"Basically, what happens is, you don't get off the same way. Instead of coming out, the stuff goes through the bladder and a lot of guys freak. But it's OK, you can still do it and feel good. You just need to be cool and give yourself time."

There were some questions and nervous laughs, but I could tell they were all grateful for the intel.

When the meeting was over, Sergeant Whip waved me over to the bed. "That showed moxie. I want you to take over Intel from Duke; he's going back to the world. And one more thing." He waved me closer. "See what you can do about Maverick."

* * *

It was another day before Duke and I were both free to talk, and I used the time to work on Eddie.

I said, "Hey, Maverick. *"Sick is sick / No test / No punishment / Not the pre-season / For Better Days."*

"You think you're so smart," he said.

"That poet was a maverick. And Big Boy G was tough, he could take it."

"He wasn't going to be pushed around," said Eddie. "So he took off."

"But he didn't wimp out. He went the distance."

"You're twisting this," said Eddie. He pulled the covers over his head.

I was getting to him.

Duke was in a good mood. He was leaving in two days.

I asked him about this name thing.

"Whip thinks everybody needs a fighting name in this place," he said. "Makes you brave."

"Who named him Whip?"

"He named himself, years ago when he was playing a video game called Fire Team Alpha."

"Years ago? When he was in the Marines?"

Duke rolled his eyes. "Whip's hardly ever been anywhere but here since he was fourteen. He's Stage III. It's everywhere, and it keeps recurring. His kidneys are shot and his heart's leaky."

"So why is Eddie such a big deal to Whip?"

"He fixates on Eddie so he doesn't have to think about himself," said Duke. "Could be a symbol. If he can pull Eddie through, maybe he can make it."

I was impressed. No wonder Duke was Intel. "How do you know so much?"

"Eavesdropping. If you look real sick and hunch over, doctors and nurses talk like you aren't there. Anything else?"

"Yeah. Why doesn't Whip give me a name?"

"He thinks he sees something in you but he's not sure yet. He doesn't want to make another mistake like Maverick."

"That's not a mistake yet."

Duke looked me over. "You got a plan?"

"Maybe."

Eavesdropping was easy. Part of recovering from the RND was getting your muscles and your gastrointestinal system moving again, and the best way to do that was walking laps around the floor, about twenty to the mile, I figured. You passed the nurses' station twice each lap, and after a few passes they didn't notice you anymore. Even if you stopped, you were invisible to them. You could listen to nurses and doctors talking among themselves or on the telephone. You could peek into charts and records. I got good at it, wheeling around the floor with my IV stand, stopping to pretend to rest as I sneaked quick glances.

I found out a lot. Whip's real name was Wayne, and

he'd been a patient for almost eight years, and he'd had every kind of surgery and radiation and chemo they had. It worked for a while and then it didn't.

Most of the guys were doing OK. Some were sicker than others and some had a tougher time with the chemo.

And then there was Eddie. The shrinks had been working on him, but they weren't getting anywhere. There were psychological terms I didn't understand, but it all seemed to come down to Eddie having backed himself into a corner. They couldn't talk him out.

I said to Eddie, "I hear they're going to throw you out because they need your bed for somebody who wants to live."

He sneered at me. *"Some things are worse / Than death."*

I was ready for him with the next three lines. *"But until you've tried them / After death / Who knows?"* That knocked him back. While he was reeling, I said, "There's your problem, Eddie, you don't go all the way. You didn't even know the whole stanza."

There was no ceremony when Duke shipped out; he just shook hands and split. I thought he might ask me about Eddie, but his mind was already in the real world. At the elevator, I heard his dad call him David.

"I've watched a lot of guys leave here," said Sergeant Whip. "A few come back for a second tour." He seemed crumpled in the wheelchair, his sharp features somehow softer. "Making any progress with Maverick?"

"I think so." That seemed to perk him up. "I'm trying to get at him through poetry."

"Poetry. Never would have thought of that."

My parents and the oncologists met at my bed and talked over me. They had decided on a protocol. They would start me on a week of chemo in the hospital, then two weeks off, then on and off as an outpatient. Will Sea. But they sounded positive.

When they left, I said to Eddie, "We could go through chemo together."

"Like holding hands?" he sneered.

"Superman lent me his cape / Didn't fit / Had to weave my own."

Eddie stared up at the ceiling for a long time. Then he said, "Dr. Kenny hates me. He'd never let it happen."

Eavesdropping at the nurses' station, I realized I had only one more day before Eddie would be discharged unless he agreed to treatment.

I needed some advice. But the shrinks and the Fellows

wouldn't talk to me about Eddie, and Duke was gone and Whip mostly slept. I was on my own.

I needed to show some moxie.

I sat down on Eddie's bed and shut off his TV. I couldn't tell if he was annoyed or scared of me.

"I think you never really understood that B. B. Goings poem. You thought it was about a guy who quit. It was really about a guy who wouldn't give up."

"Big Boy G dies at the end," he said.

"Says who?" I said.

"He drowns, swimming toward the horizon."

"That's your interpretation, and I think it's wrong. *'Now a bobbing speck on the Will Sea.'* He's still out there, never giving up, trying to get to the other side."

There were tears in Eddie's eyes. "We'd do chemo together?"

"What do you say?"

"What about that Fire Team Bravo crap?"

"We'll see," I said. "Yes or no?"

He said, *"From steely dreams / Here I come."*

Sounded like a yes to me.

I went up to the lounge on the roof, found a quiet corner, and paged through the poetry textbook. The poet that B. B. Goings was supposed to wanna be, e. e. cummings, who only wrote in lowercase, was pretty good, too.

Harder to understand than old B. B., but his poems were funny and full of life. Be good to read them during chemo.

The Fire Team took Whip to the OR. We started tapping just before we hit the doors, chanting, "Kill Cancer." Whip said to me, "Intel, you're Acting Leader till I get back."

"Me?" I said.

"You got moxie. If I don't come back you're Sergeant Moxie."

"You'll be back."

"Better believe it, troop."

"Outstanding," I said.

It was the last time we saw him. We knew before they rolled up his bed. Eavesdropping, I found out that his kidneys failed on the table, and then one by one his major systems shut down until his big leaky heart stopped beating.

The new kid was thin, shaky. I waited while his parents hugged him good-bye and Nurse Laurel settled him in with Tank and the Fellows interrogated him. Then I moved in.

"Welcome to Fire Team Bravo," I said, grabbing his hand and pumping it. "I'm Sergeant Moxie, your team leader."

"What?" He stared at me.

"Team means you're not alone, brothers got your back."

He snarled, "Get out."

"I like that—you're a fighter. All you need to know right now is that cancer can kill you, but you don't have to kiss its butt. Later I'll give you some poems to read. What's your name?"

His mouth was so dry his tongue clicked. Scared spitless. "Conor."

"What kind of name is that?" said my Intel chief, Maverick.

"We'll fix it," I said.

ABOUT THE AUTHOR AND THE STORY

Along with his reputation as a *New York Times* sports reporter and columnist, a television interviewer, and a writer of nonfiction and fiction for adults, Robert Lipsyte is one of the most important figures in the world of young adult literature. His first young adult novel, *The Contender,* has been considered a classic in the field since its publication in 1967. And he continues to create books that entertain, inform, and challenge teenage readers. His most recent publications include the insightful *Heroes of Baseball* as well as the fictional *Raiders Night*, featuring the co-captain of a high school football team who has to face up to a demanding father, a vindictive girlfriend, his use of steroids, and the other co-captain's rape of a rookie teammate. Among his other publications are *One Fat Summer; Yellow Flag; The Brave; The Chief; Warrior Angel; Assignment, Sports;* and *Free to Be Muhammad Ali.*

Recognizing his outstanding contributions to young adult literature, the Assembly on Literature for Adolescents of the National Council of Teachers of English presented Robert Lipsyte with the ALAN Award in 1999, and the American Library Association honored him in 2001 with a prestigious Margaret A. Edwards Award. He received the Meyer Berger Award for Distinguished Reporting (twice) from Columbia University and an Emmy Award for On-Camera Achievement for *The Eleventh Hour* television program. He was also a runner-up for the Pulitzer Prize in commentary.

Like the hospitalized characters in "Let's Hear It for Fire Team Bravo," Bob Lipsyte is a survivor of testicular cancer. "The good news about testicular cancer," says Lipsyte, who wrote about his experiences with the disease in *In the Country of Illness: Comfort and Advice for the Journey,* "is that it is usually curable and that new drugs have greatly reduced such side effects of chemotherapy as fatigue and nausea. The better news is that every man can take charge of his own exam. I'd suggest that once a month after your fifteenth birthday, roll each testicle gently between the thumbs and fingers of both hands, particularly feeling for a small growth attached to the outside of the testicle. A swollen testicle or one that feels harder or more tender than usual are other reasons to see a urologist. Most pain and swelling in the area is not cancer, but why take a chance when early detection can make an enormous difference in the extent, discomfort, and inconvenience of treatment?"